L2YALTIES
PART

VONTEZ

DESTINY'S PUBLICATIONS

L2YALTIES

PART

VONTEZ

Destiny's Publications
P.O. Box 24362
Cincinnati, OH 45224-9998

This book is a work of fiction. Names, characters, places and incidents are products of the author's imagination or are used fictitiously. Any resemblance to actual events or locales or persons, living or dead, is entirely coincidental.

©2018 by Ronald Vontez Williams

Cover design: Consandra Wright

10 9 8 7 6 5 4 3 2 1

Manufactured in the United States of America
ISBN: 978-0-692-17980-2

Dedication

This book is dedicated to my children; Ronesha, Nyshayla, Ronald Logan, and Destiny. The four of you are my inspiration, and the combustible materials that fuel my drive and determination to be all that I am. You all are my lineage, and it is my responsibility to leave you with a legacy. If I could leave you with one quote to live by, it would be:

"You can be anything you want to be in this world. All you have to do is try!" - VONTEZ

Chapter 1

Months had passed since the debacle of what was supposed to be the imminent demise of "Snake", which had taken an inconceivable turn for the worse, leaving one of the assigned hitmen dead and the other one locked up in a maximum security prison with a 25 to life prison sentence.

It was now April of 2015. Spring being the season for new wildlife and foliage, it was the perfect setting for Vontez's judicial release from prison. Vontez's lawyer had been successful in his efforts to obtain his freedom at the request of his two women, Stephanie and Keisha. He left prison with new vigor and resolution, determined to make the most of his second chance at life. Something had sparked inside of him, after hearing a sermon in church about "purpose". Vontez was adamant about making some changes in his life. Overcoming the unyielding force of "karma" would be his biggest obstacle.

His mother and two girlfriends were planning a welcome home party for their recently released loved one. Mama V would take the lead on organizing the gathering, with the assistance of Verdale making phone calls to assemble Vontez's friends for the function. Stephanie and Keisha made sure that the nucleus of the Urban Styles staff was in attendance, as well as his business partners from the sports agency, Louis and Bernard, along with their former teammate, Lamont Green.

It was Saturday, April 18th and Vontez had gone to court the previous day for his judicial release hearing. Stephanie and Keisha were in attendance, along with his lawyer. Mama V and Verdale had been informed that the hearing was merely a formality and that Vontez would be released that evening, so they opted to not attend in person. A banquet hall was rented immediately, after hearing the news of Vontez's liberation date for the following day. Mama V and Verdale already knew that the night of his release belonged to his ladies.

Stephanie and Keisha sat in the back of the courtroom while the judge laid out the terms of the judicial release to Vontez in great detail. After listening intently to the information Vontez was led back to the County holding tank. He would be released in a few hours, pending paperwork. His two women waited anxiously for over three hours in the lobby of the Hamilton County Justice Center before they saw Vontez emerge from the dark recesses of the hallway that led to the processing department of the building wearing a gray sweatshirt and state issued shoes. Vontez's chiseled frame and glowing skin had both women salivating with thoughts of caressing and tasting their man. They both rushed up to him, meeting in an embrace that was long overdue. Vontez tongue kissed each woman passionately before they all left the building hand in hand.

As if it were scripted, when the trio reached Keisha's silver BMW X5 with the tinted windows, she hit the keyless entry button on her key fob and Vontez and Stephanie entered the back seat of the luxury crossover vehicle. Before Keisha could pull away from the parking space, Vontez's sweatpants were pulled down and Stephanie's face was planted in his lap.

"Damn I missed y'all!" Vontez expressed to his women as Stephanie continued to pleasure him.

"We missed you too Papi!" Keisha replied first.

"Umm, yes Papi we missed you and Moby!" Stephanie managed to say as she momentarily removed Vontez's bell head from the confines of her water mouth.

Vontez slips his hand under Stephanie's skirt to move her panties to the side, in order to play with her pussy, only to find that she isn't wearing any. He then slides his middle finger into her leaking wet *love crevice*. Stephanie lets out a sensuous seductive moan, making her jaws tighten around the girth of Vontez's manhood. Keisha, as if she were a professional coach or something starts to vocally orchestrate the sexual exploits of her two lovers.

"Stroke that tight juicy pussy Papi! See how tight we kept that pussy for ya Papi! Mine is just as tight Papi" Keisha verbalizes.

"Yeah, I feel how tight my pussy is," Vontez says as he strokes in and out of Stephanie's *seeping monkey*.

"Show Papi how much we missed him," Keisha instructs Stephanie. She continues as the couple in the backseat goes at it more intensely, "taste how fresh that pussy is Papi!" she directs Vontez. He takes his soaked fingers out of Stephanie and licks them clean.

"Let me taste Papi", Keisha asked Vontez and he strokes Stephanie a few more times with his middle and index fingers. He removed the dripping wet appendages and extends his hand to the driver's seat. Keisha turns her head over her right shoulder and erotically envelops his moist fingers in her mouth, tasting the sweet secretions of their shared lover.

"Uumh Umm!" she says animatedly. Their ride home was filled with an abundance of lustful sounds.

When they arrived at their residence in Mason, a suburb on the outskirts of Cincinnati, Keisha's pussy was soaking wet from the anticipation of her turn to taste Vontez. She turns into their driveway and clicked the garage door opener attached to the sun visor.

"We're home guys!" she announces as she brings Vontez and Stephanie out of their salacious daze.

Stephanie raises her head, removing Vontez's throbbing manhood from her mouth and grabs the hand that he just removed from her drenched pussy and sucked every molecule of moisture from his hand. Vontez pulls up his sweatpants and glanced around the three car garage. He looked to his right and saw Stephanie's Black BMW X5, and next to it he saw a brand new cocaine white BMW 760LI with a red bow on the roof.

"Ahh, hell naw! No y'all didn't! Girls I love it!" he exclaims.

"We knew you would", says Stephanie.

"Papi, you know we had to upgrade you. The other one was 2 years old! Nothing but the best for a Boss like you Papi!" adds Keisha.

"That's what's up ladies! Y'all are too much!" says Vontez.

After looking over and admiring his new lavish form of transportation, the trio enters into their home through the door attached to the garage. Vontez pauses momentarily to admire the plush décor of his home, which he hadn't seen in roughly 2 years. Stephanie grabs a silver platter from a kitchen drawer that had some 'Girl Scout Cookies' marijuana strand on it, and begins to twist one up. Vontez has a seat on a stool at the island counter in the middle of the kitchen. Keisha goes over to the bar located in the far corner of the living room and returns to the kitchen area with a bottle of "1738" and three shot glasses. She pours three shots and Vontez stands up and says, "I want to propose a toast! I want to propose a toast to my ladies for always holding me down, for being there for me through thick and thin, and for being two living examples that "Loyalty is Royalty". I love you both with all my heart!" Vontez raises his glass and shouts, "Cheers!", and the girls both chime in. After a few more shots and a few moments of the girls smoking their blunt of the very powerful medical marijuana, the lovers make their way up the stairs.

Once in their bedroom, clothes immediately go flying off their bodies. Vontez lays across the California King sized pillow-top mattress taking time to view his two sexy vixens with veneration.

"Oh my God we've been waiting on this moment Papi!" says Keisha as both women stare at Vontez's hardened, twitching love stick.

The ladies play one round of a twisted game of Rock, Paper, Scissors with Stephanie displaying the symbol for "rock", and Keisha displaying her hand flat like a piece of paper. "Paper covers Rock!" she says flirtatiously and kisses Stephanie as they both walk towards their man.

They continue to kiss while both drop their heads toward Vontez's ever hardening penis, until their mouths meet at the tip of his bell head. They both lick and kiss each side of his manhood, up and down from the tip of his dick head to the bottom of his balls. Keisha takes him in her mouth twirling her tongue around the circumference of him, while taking his length to the back of her throat. Stephanie simultaneously softly sucks his balls and strokes his shaft in and out of Keisha's drooling mouth.

After 15 minutes of orally pleasing Vontez, teasingly stopping each time before he came, the women reposition themselves. Stephanie and Keisha both three-way kiss Vontez before taking up new positions. Stephanie straddles Vontez's face backwards tooting her ass in the air with her hands on his chest, allowing him to lick and suck her dripping pussy from the back. Keisha climbs on Vontez's lap facing Stephanie, and inserts his impressive *"love tool"* inside of her. She shrieks as the head hits the G-spot at the back of her pussy walls. The triad of lovers continues in the enjoyment of one another for hours, until all parties involved were exhausted beyond belief.

Upon awakening from the desirable events of the previous night, Vontez looks over at his women, one asleep on each side of him and mouths the words, "Thank You for giving me my life back" to his Lord and Savior. He looks over at the alarm clock and observes the time. The digital clock read 11:42am. Vontez stretched for the first time in 2 years, waking up a free man. He leaned to his left then to his right giving each woman a kiss on the forehead waking them up. "What time do we have to be there?" (Referring to the banquet hall) he poses the question to no one in particular.

Keisha responds first, "at 1 o'clock", without opening her eyes.

Stephanie chimes in, "what time is it?" Vontez replies, "a quarter to 12."

The women began to move about, gaining consciousness from their ferocious love making induced slumber. The trio scrambles to take showers, brush their teeth and pick out their coordinating white linen outfits. Vontez popped the tags off his two piece linen outfit that his two women meticulously picked out and purchased for him, as the women curled and styled each other's hair, something that was an added bonus since both women were master cosmetologists. Vontez was anxious to see his family, especially his children. Once dressed they all took final looks in the mirror admiring the beauty that they all possessed and headed downstairs.

Stephanie began rolling up, while Keisha poured shots of liquor, and Vontez pulled the new Beamer out of the garage. He comes back into the house to get the women and they all take a shot before arming the house alarm and exiting their home. Both women sit in the backseat of the luxury vehicle and Vontez chauffeurs his two divas to his "Homecoming" banquet.

They informed him of the location of the Marquee Banquet Hall and they begin their journey. Everyone had arrived at the Hall by 12:45pm, under the direct orders of Mama V. Vontez pulls into the packed parking lot of the Marquee and is instantly overwhelmed by the spectacular turnout of supporters and family.

"Damn it's a lot of people here!" he said in astonishment.

"Yes Papi and they're all here for you!" replies Keisha.

"Baby you know that you got a lot of love out here, and people are really happy you are back home!" adds Stephanie.

"Yeah, I realize that now. Sometimes when you're locked up and the letters don't come as often as you would like, and the visits slow down, you lose sight of that. But I understand that when you're free, life can sometimes get in the way. So I'm just happy to see all the love now", he says.

The trio gather themselves mentally to face the crowd. The women check each other's make up and primp each other's hair one last time. Once satisfied with each other's looks, they turn their attention to their man. Brushing off his shoulders, lightly tugging on his shirt at the bottom to straighten out the slight wrinkles that had formed in the linen from sitting in the car, and finally wiping the beads of sweat from the bridge of his nose.

The three coordinating individuals make their way to the front entrance of the hall where they are immediately spotted by Vontez's business partners who were outside smoking cigars.

"Ahh shit! Look at my man, looking like new money! What up Tez?" blurts out Bernard as he sees Vontez turn the corner.

"That's my dawg! That's my dawg!" Sweet Lou says in his best "Chris Tucker" voice.

"My niggas!" Vontez says animatedly and he daps and hugs the two men. The three men separate and form a circle, with each man putting in their right hand. Vontez yells out, "Am I my brother's keeper?"

"Yes I am!" Bernard and Louis yell back in unison.

Vontez repeats "Am I my brother's keeper?"

"Yes I am!" The two men repeat again, and they break their huddle as if they were on the grid iron green once again.

"Damn it's good to see y'all!" Vontez says with emotion in his voice.

"Bruh, it's good to have you back home" replies Sweet Lou.

"Yes it is! The three Amigos back together again", adds Bernard.

Bernard and Louis butt out their cigars and follow behind Vontez and his ladies as they enter into the building. "Daddy, Daddy!" screams Vontez's four children as they run up to him, with his youngest daughter, Trinity jumping into his arms.

"Wow look at y'all! Y'all done got so big!" Vontez remarks as he embraces his offspring.

The children and their father express their love and affection for one another with family members, including Stephanie and Keisha, snapping photos to capture the moments of their reunion to later be posted on Instagram and Facebook for all to relive. Vontez enters the main room of the banquet hall, still holding his youngest daughter and draped by his other children, followed closely behind by his two sexy divas. The room explodes in applause as he enters.

Vontez is overwhelmed and overcome with joy from the emotion and show of love from his family, friends and associates. He walks to the center of the room where Mama V and Verdale are standing with a microphone. Mama V says with tears running down her face, "Welcome Home Baby! I love you so much!" Vontez eases Trinity down from his arms and hugs his mother tightly. He loosens his embrace and looks her in her watery eyes and says,

"I'm sorry mama. I won't' disappoint you again, I promise!"

"Baby we'll talk about that later. Let's just enjoy you being home," and she kisses him on the cheek before releasing her hug.

Vontez looks up to see his smiling brother and they share an embrace before he hands the microphone to Vontez. The next few hours were filled with love, music and laughter amongst the family and friends as they celebrated the return home of the man of the hour.

Chapter 2

"Inmate Carter #577906 report to the visiting room!" sternly said the guard who processed the visitors for the Federal Penitentiary Intake, located in rural Greenville, Illinois. His instructions echoed over the P.A system that could be heard throughout the concrete and steel fortress. E-Tone put on his winter green federal uniform that he pressed to perfection the night before, anticipating the visit from his wife, Samantha, and his lawyer Harvey Wienstein. He stepped into his Timberland boots and laced them up. Finally, he grabbed his soft-bristle brush and brushed his hair in a 360 degree direction, causing a cascading wave pattern to be more prominent.

He left the confines of his one-man cell and went to the "sally-port", indicating to the C.O. in charge of his pod, that he had a visit. Once the C.O. popped the lock on the "pod" door, E-

Tone entered the hallway. He turned left and walked down the long hallway and hit the buzzer located to the right of the visiting room door. He waited to hear the buzz sound indicating that the security lock had been released, and then he opened the steel door.

"You Carter?" asked the C.O.

"Yeah", E-Tone responds.

"What's your inmate#?" asks the officer.

"#577906!" E-Tone bellows.

The officer looks up and examines the inmate that stood before him, taking notice of his accessories. He talks aloud as he jots down the information "(1) pair of Timberland boots, (1) brown belt. Do you have (1) tee shirt and (1) pair of undershorts and (1) pair of socks?" the C.O. nonchalantly asks E-Tone.

"Yes Sir!" answers a growingly impatient E-tone.

"Alright, well your visitors are out there, just sit across from them. You are permitted a brief kiss and a hug in the beginning and the end of the visit. You are allowed to hold hands across the table only. If at any time during the visit, the visiting room C.O. suspects suspicious activity, your visit will be terminated. Do you understand?" the laid back officer says with a more authoritative tone.

"Yes Sir!" responds E-Tone.

After receiving his final visiting instructions, E-Tone opens the door leading to the visiting area. He pans the room to find his wife and lawyer at the very first table, closest to the vending machines. Samantha and E-Tones eyes met and they both smiled. It had been over two months since she last saw him at his sentencing court appearance. Samantha instantly notices that he is returning to his normal weight. E-Tone had lost a substantial amount of weight after being shot, and having to wear a colostomy bag for three months while his intestines healed.

When reaching the table, Samantha stands and affectionately hugs and kisses her deeply missed husband. They embrace momentarily since E-Tone was being cautious not to hug too long, so his visit would not be terminated. After releasing his wife from his loving grasp, he extends his hand toward his expensive attorney.

"How's it going Eric?" the older, gray haired, Jewish lawyer concernedly asks.

"A lot better! I've been eating solid food for 7, going on 8 weeks now and I've gained 17lbs back. I feel pretty good under the circumstances. What's the good news?" E-Tone says as they all sit down at their assigned table.

"You know me all too well my friend," the sly lawyer says with a light chuckle before he continues.

"Well my friend, I put in an appeal of your case after I received the Motion-to-Discover evidence file. It seems as though in all the "unsolved" homicides that you were charged with, the ballistics show that each of the victims were either killed by their own weapons or your partner's shotgun. The

14

weapons retrieved from you at the time of your arrest and crime scene were surprisingly clean, and I thought I was crafty. You could have been charged with attempted "armed robbery", but in their haste to pin the murders on you, armed robbery charges were never filed. The federal prosecutors fucked up.....royally! And after I get through with them they are gonna owe you big time for violating your civil rights with their "fast & speedy" railroaded trial! Give me a month or so and you should be back at home with Ms. Samantha and your son!" the old veteran lawyer finishes his statement with utter confidence.

"Now that's what I'm talking about, it don't get no better than that! And them *muthafuckas* gonna owe me when we get done with this shit! Now that's what's up!" E-Tone says emphatically as he squeezes Samantha's hand across the visiting room table.

"Well your associate paid for the best and that's what you got my friend; the best damn Federal Attorney that money can buy!" Weinstein says referring to Verdale, who had hired the accomplished attorney at his own expense.

Verdale and Vontez were all about loyalty. E-Tone and J.J. had been riding with them for years and they appreciated having "wolves" on their team. Plus, they knew that if they had left E-Tone to hang out to dry, he could have sunk their ship. He knew too much vital information to just toss to the waste-side. After a couple of hours of lively conversation, E-Tone and Samantha said their goodbyes, culminating in an impassioned hug and kiss.

Harvey Weinstein extended his hand for E-Tone to shake and said, "See you on the other side my friend."

E-Tone shook his head and said "Yes you will."

E-Tone, gleaming with happiness on his way back to his cell, was instantly elevated as thoughts of revenge infused his mind. He thought to himself that Candy and Sapphire would never see him coming. He smiled with a devilish grin as he laid down on the federal penitentiary wool blanket that draped over his firm mattress.

Meanwhile, back in Louisville....

Sapphire was entering the 3rd trimester of her pregnancy. She and Jerome had a beautiful spring wedding ceremony. Sapphire was a gorgeous glowing bride, even with her protruding belly. Candy, as her maid of honor and the other female bar employees as her bridesmaids, filled the wedding party with attractive women who shared in the storybook romance of their friend. Fittingly, Candy caught the bouquet at the wedding reception. Candy and Snake had a late summer wedding planned. Candy figured that Sapphire should have given birth by her wedding date at the end of August, and was considering a destination wedding in the Caribbean.

Snake and Candy had grown increasingly close since their collusion that brought down the forces of evil that were plotting his demise. Business was booming at the club and the annual

"Kentucky Derby" was approaching by weeks end. The "Snake Pit" would be jumping for sure this weekend. Radio spots flooded the air waves as out-of-state visitors trickled into town, informing them that the "Snake Pit" was the place to be. In addition to the club, the couples had ventured off into the concert promoting business. After recent events that they had narrowly and luckily escaped unscaved, they were looking to totally legitimize their endeavors. The women had given up their shared condo to move in with their partners of the opposite sex. Along with their hearts, their actions showed where their loyalty lied.

In preparation for the weekend events, the couples were discussing whether or not to have the hottest local artist, "Peanut", perform his smash hit single *"Lil Mama"* at the club on Saturday.

"I thought we was going for the grown and sexy look? An artist on the R&B and Neo-Soul side. I'm not sure about this "Peanut" character!" a reluctant Jerome says emphatically.

"I know..... I was thinking the same thing at first, but this isn't going to be our target audience all the time. Most of the out of town folks coming in are going to be younger. My guess is between the ages of 18-25yrs old, and they are going to kick it up and down Broadway all day. At night, the young cats are going to be wherever the young ladies are going to be. Believe it or not, this "Peanut" character is going to bring the young ladies out!" an assured Snake says confidently.

"I agree!" adds a convinced Candy. She continues "that song *"Lil Mama"* is my jam!" Sapphire chimes in, "that song is hot and that hook is fire. *Gone drop it lil mama, gone make that cheese, gone pop it lil mama, gone twerk for me*," she says, and she and Candy begin to laugh.

"See what I'm talkin *bout*! That song even got our girls wantin to shake they ass!" Snake exclaims to Jerome.

"Damn I see! Babe you gone twerk junior right on out here in the office," Jerome playfully says to his lady, and Sapphire playfully stands in front of him and pops and claps her booty in her newly wedded husbands face, as the group laughs.

"Well, I'll confirm with his manager and get him added to the radio spots today. A good 4 or 5 days of advertising will do the job. Once they hear that "Peanut" will be here, it's really gonna be jumping!" Snake says with excitement in his voice.

After the small talk and chit-chat, the couples leave the confines of the back office and head out for lunch at the Olive Garden on the riverfront.

Chapter 3

"What's up Bruh, I'm outside!"

"Alright, I'll be right out" answers Vontez.

After being home for over a week, the two brothers finally had the opportunity to talk so Verdale could bring Vontez up to speed on the organization's plans and activities. Vontez said his goodbyes to his two adoring women and left the comfort of his luxurious home. Wearing a form fitting black tee, camouflage cargo shorts, and a pair of black retro Air Jordans, his attire was simple and comfortable. Although the only jewelry that he wore was a stainless steel Movado watch with a black face, his presence and swagger let you know that he was a man of

Vontez entered his brother's pearl white Cadillac Escalade, "Yeah Bruh Bruh, I like this here! Plush ass seats, the rear view camera, the navigation system, crisp clean Bose sound system and the wood-grain is classic D-Boy shit. Yeah I like this!" Vontez expresses to his younger brother.

"Good looking out big bruh!" replies Verdale.

"So what's up with the expansion move down south? Do you think Tae and "Lil Dee" can handle that shit?" Vontez poses the question to his brother and now business partner, already knowing the answer.

Vontez had schooled the two men years ago when they began their hustling exploits, and both men took to the game like fish to water. Verdale gave his brother one of those "come on man" type of looks and pulled off from the residential area before answering him.

"Come on bruh, these two *muthafuckas* got your seal of approval written all over them!" he states to his older brother.

"Yeah I know, I'm just fucking with you bruh." Vontez says humorously as he continues, "Yeah, both of them cats are thoroughbreds and they can handle shit down south. I ain't got no problem with that. But we gonna have to sit down with yo boy Flash again cause I know we can get that ticket down to about "ten racks" a piece for a brick, especially since that'll be 450 units a month. I know that he can do better than the "twelve-five" he talkin *bout*", Vontez finishes.

"I was thinking the same thing, but I figured since some were consignment, that it was fair. I think you can convince him otherwise. After all, this is a money making move for all of us" Verdale adds.

"I think we can make that happen. Looks like we'll be flying out to Vegas real soon, but check this out lil bruh..... I've been done some serious soul searching. Although I'm a *hustla* to the core, I've been thinking about taking a back seat on this shit, my heart ain't in it like that no more. I'm gonna be here to help consult you on some shit, but I think you can handle the role. I mean on some real shit, since I've been gone, you've already been holdin it down. What you think about that lil bruh?" Vontez sincerely asks his younger brother.

"I ain't gotta problem *wit* that! We'll still run this shit together; you'll just be falling back on the visibility part. I ain't trippin bruh. You know I kinda like this shit fo'real!" an excited Verdale blurts out.

"I'm still on papers because of this judicial release shit, but it's gonna help me tighten my shit up. Plus, I gotta find my true purpose out here bruh. I feel like God got some more stuff planned for my life. I just gotta figure this shit out, but, I am gonna help get this expansion finalized for us though. After that shit happened with E-Tone and the homeboy J.J., I've really been thinking long and hard about this game. You know I did some crazy shit in my day and ain't never had a problem with *"puttin in werk"*, but I guess I must be gettin soft in my old age or something", a genuine Vontez exclaims.

"Nigga you ain't getting old, you just getting wise", Verdale says with a smile.

"Do you think we should even do this expansion? Shit! Do you think we should even continue this shit?" Vontez asks with concern.

21

"It's up to you big bruh. I was just picking up the slack until you got back home fa real. We got options, you just say the word", Verdale says to his brother with conviction in his heart.

"See, that's one of my dilemmas lil bruh. You and I do have options, but the hundreds of *muthafuckas* that depend on us don't.....and you saw "Superfly"! The minute niggas know that you thinking about bowing out the game and leave they asses hangin, that's when the wolves start gunning for your ass on some real shit! We gonna go thru with the expansion, get everybody comfortable first and then if everything go right, we'll put the right *muthafuckas* in the right positions. Just keep cool and go on with business as usual," a convincing Vontez tells his brother.

"That's what's up. Hey, I got a good ass federal lawyer for our boy E-Tone. This cat named Wienstien, Harvey Weinstein, and he says that the shit looks promising too!" Verdale states to his brother.

"That's what's up! Shit, one thing I know about E-Tone is he ain't gonna let that shit slide so Snake and that scandalous bitch betta watch out if they cut his ass loose," Vontez boldly exclaims.

The two brothers rode around for a while discussing business and catching up on the latest occurrences in the city before stopping to get lunch at their favorite restaurant, "Benihanas". The rest of the afternoon was filled with shopping and "shit talking" between the two charismatic brothers. Unbeknownst to them, the brothers were being tailed all afternoon. At every stop and destination, a dark colored vehicle remained equidistant from them. A shadowy figure, with a high powered digital camera continuously snapped shot after shot of the two brothers while they unawaringly entered and exited multiple stores.

Chapter 4

Saturday, May 2nd had arrived and sports fans around the country were in full frenzy. The NBA Playoffs were in full swing, the annual Kentucky Derby was hours away, and later that evening the most anticipated fight of the decade would finally be taking place. Floyd "Money" Mayweather and Manny Pacquiao would at last square off in a battle for the ages. Snake and Jerome had agreed that the concert portion of the evening would take place from 9pm until the main event fight started around 10:30pm, and after the fight ended, the guest DJ, "DJ Inferno" would blaze the turntables for the rest of the evening. Precious and Monique were going over the bartending procedures once again, with the newly hired bartender "Fawn", in anticipation of the hectic night. Candy and Sapphire no longer worked at the bar in the same capacity, for more than obvious reasons, but they were still actively participating in the preparations for the night festivities.

The "Snake Pit" was revealing their newly constructed, fenced in patio addition for the first time and the two best friends, and soon to be cousins, were instructing workers where to place Tiki torches and bug zapping lanterns on the patio. With the addition of the patio, the bar could easily hold an additional 100-150 more people. In addition to the patio being added, the two cousins had invested in a food truck that would stay posted on the premises, adding extra revenue to their growing legal empire. Two of Jerome's three sisters and their husbands were operating the food truck for their family. Juanita would take the food orders and handle the money, Joyce would handle all of the cold items such as coleslaw, potato salad and beverages, while their husbands, Larry and Calvin, would cook the chicken, fish and french fries.

The afternoon turned to evening before they knew it and the city of Louisville was a lively as it had been in years. The crowd at the bar was increasing with each passing moment. Out-of-towners and locals alike were giddy at the expectation of the young rap sensation "Peanut's" performance at the "Snake Pit". Luke and Tiny were working the door and had things running in an orderly fashion. Virgil and Chubb's were doing security inside the club and manning the patio. Although it was just the first week of May, it was unseasonably warm. The temperature was still in the low eighties by nightfall, and the ladies were skimpily dressed for the weather and the occasion.

"Girl, where y'all at? The lil nigga "Peanut" about to hit the stage in about 5 minutes and it's thick as hell up in here!" Candy informs Sapphire after reaching her on her cellphone.

"We should be there in 5 or 10 minutes. You know how this traffic is on Broadway, especially this weekend" Sapphire replies.

"Ok, well see y'all in a minute then" Candy utters before hanging up from the phone call.

Sapphire and Jerome pulled up at the bar to find a crowd of people in the parking lot. The radio station's van was parked out front because they were doing a live remote from the club. The line was as long as Jerome and Sapphire had ever seen, and the parking lot scene was jumpin like the "93 Freak—Nick". The radio spots they had on "104.3 the Heat" had definitely done the job, plus the "semi-cult" following "Peanut" had developed, had the "Snake Pit" pegged as the place to be in the city on Derby Night 2015.

"Damn Babe! We done had some crowds before but I ain't never seen this *muthafucka* this *off the chain*!" Jerome exclaims to his newly wedded wife.

"I know Romey! They say be careful what you ask for and wow! We wanted a crowd and we *sho' nuff* got one tonight," Sapphire retorts in response to her husband's comments.

After parking in their reserved spot, the couple makes their way inside of the crowed club. They both exchanged greetings with Luke and Tiny before gaining entrance passed the frenzy of party goers. Making their way to the side of the bar, they find Candy and Snake. The two cousins exchange pounds, the ladies exchange sisterly hugs, and they all turn their attention to the stage as "Peanut's" hype man introduces him to the crowd.

"Ladies and Gentleman it's the man who brought you the underground classics, *"Duelly's on my Caprice"* and *"She got that wet-wet"*, the man that talk *mo* shit than the greatest and got *mo* swag than the latest! The man that niggas fuck *wit* and the bitches wanna fuck! The man who brought you the latest strip club anthem *"Lil Mama"*! Give it up for Louisville's own but soon to be internationally known "Peanut". The young rapper takes the stage to the amped up crowd's approval, and put on a show that rivaled a "Lil Wayne" Grammy performance. Every young lady in the club was reciting the *"Lil Mama"* hook like it was their favorite nursery rhyme, and the fellas were grindin up on them as they twerked and shook their asses to the infectious beat of the song.

The preliminary fights were being shown on the flat screens throughout the bar hyping up the already "turned up" young thugs in the building. "Peanut" ended his set as the Mayweather and Pacquiao introductions were being announced. The crowd's attentions turned to the flat screens that were hung throughout the club, including the patio area. Weed smoke hung in the air like tempestuous clouds before a storm. Bets were being brokered by young hustlers who weren't students of the sweet science of boxing. With lofty notions of a big payday, one young D-Boy in particular was taking all bets which were rolling in by the opening bell, because he was betting on the underdog, Manny Pacquiao.

The fight was an instant classic with both fighters bringing their best efforts to the table. The fight went the distance and the crowd was awaiting the judge's decision with great anticipation. Shit talking was exchanged back and forth between opposing betters. The crowd quieted as the ring announcer read the score cards.

"Let's give it up for our two main event boxers this evening for putting on one *hellava* show folks! Let's give 'em a round of applause! (The crowd obliges) Judge #1 scores the fight 116-112 and judges #2 & #3 score the fight 115-113….and your winner by a unanimous decision and still undefeated "Pretty Boy" Floyd Mayweather Jr!"

The crowd both on TV and in the bar erupts in a cascade of cheers and boos after the decision was broadcasted by the announcer. As the betters settled their debts, a disturbance could be heard in the far corner of the bar.

"Pay up *muthafucka*! You heard the decision Nigga! How you gonna bet against "Money Mayweather" any *muthafuckin* way", one of the betters said to the young *D-Boy* who had taken 7 or 8 bets against Mayweather.

"Fuck you and the rest of the *muthafuckas* I bet! This fight was fixed! Ain't no way Floyd beat Pacquiao! It should have been a draw if nothing else! I ain't *paying* y'all shit. Get it how you live *muthafucka*"! the brazin young man said and stood his ground.

Fists started flying as if they were imitating the boxers they had just watched fight. Bouncers scrambled to break up the

28

melee as the young *D-Boy* was getting the "ass whopping" he was looking for, and rightly deserved. Luke, Tiny, Virgil and Chubbs finally gained control of the crowd, tossing little niggas left and right until they ultimately pulled the last guy off the young *D-Boy* who started the whole mess in the first place.

After clearing the fight participants out of the bar, the parking lot was a swarm of stirred up bar patrons and "parking lot pimpers" who were still "*turnt* up" from the concert, fight, and derby festivities. Unsatisfied with beating the "*bet welchers*" ass, some of the unpaid agitators were still talkin shit as Luke escorted the physically and ego bruised young man to his car. Before Luke had a chance to walk away, the crowd started to sway in their direction. Feeling cornered, the beaten man emerges from his car with a 9mm in hand and lets off a few shots in the direction of the rabble-rousers. In an instant, gun fire was returned in the direction from which the gun shots were originally fired. The crowd scattered like roaches in a ghetto kitchen when the lights are turned on. Some retreated to the safety of their vehicles and screeched out of the parking lot, others ran for shelter behind the surrounding buildings and back into the bar before the doors were locked.

After the shots ceased, the bartenders, Candy, Sapphire, and the barmaids rose up from behind the bar. Others who had taken cover, including Jerome, Snake, and the security guards who had ducked down behind and underneath tables and chairs, resurfaced.

"Is everybody ok?" Snake asked in general, although looking in the direction of his fiancé.

"Yeah we good", Candy and Sapphire simultaneously answer.

Jerome runs to hold his pregnant newly wedded wife.

"Where's Luke?" Tiny yells after panning the room of its occupants.

The close-knit bar family gather themselves and led by Snake, Jerome and the rest of the security personnel make sure the coast is clear before letting the people go who had taken refuge in the bar. They exited the bar to find Luke and the young *D-Boy* who reneged on his bets, shot dead within a few feet of each other, and 3 other people wounded and being attended to by their friends in the parking lot.

Tiny yelled back in the bar direction as he ran to his friend, "Somebody call an ambulance!"

Chapter 5

"Sweet Lou! What's up my man!" Vontez greets his homeboy as he enters the sports agency.

"What's good Tez? I didn't know you was coming today," says Louis Malone, one of his partners in the business, as they give each other a pound and a hug.

"I was bored so I figured I'd just pop up on y'all. I wanted to hear more about this 2nd round pick we got now. What's his name, Logan Williams?" a high strung Vontez communicates to his friend. "Where's "B" at?" Vontez poses the question and right on que Bernard enters the office carrying two subway sandwich bags.

"Hey Tez! What's good homie?" Bernard exclaims, while sitting down the food and giving his former teammate, current business partner, and friend a brotherly hug.

"Just stopping by to holla at y'all and check on the new star signee," Vontez animatedly announces.

"Yeah we got us one for sure!" Louis chimes in.

"Let's go back to the board room and check out some of the footage from the combine," Bernard offers.

"Hey did y'all see the fight the other night? That shit was closer than what I thought it was gonna be," Vontez blurts out on the way to the boardroom.

"It's a shame it didn't happen 10 years ago when they both were in their prime," Louis acknowledges making a valid point.

"Pacquiao might have gotten in his ass a few years ago, but he done lost a step on some real shit, and he still gave ole boy all he could handle!" Bernard adds to their discussion.

The three men finish talking about the boxing match, while Bernard fires up the "Smart Board", which was a 50 inch computer screen synched to a computer tower, enabling them to watch the combine footage. After watching the impressive footage, along with some of his college highlights, Vontez was dazzled by the talented athlete that his friends and business associates were able to sign. Vontez expressed his approval to his comrades. In addition to his approval, he relayed his thoughts about auxiliary methods in sports management.

He started the dialogue with, "first of all fellas, I want to thank y'all for not only holding down the business, but for flourishing during my absence. You made some quality acquisitions and with the signing of Logan Williams, who just went early in the 2nd round, we're going to open up some eyes, but what different qualities in sports management can we bring to the table? We negotiate the contracts with their teams, we help them get settled in their respective cities by helping them buy their homes, and broker car sales with dealerships that we have relationships with, and at times we also act as assistants, scheduling flights, making reservations, and performing other miscellaneous duties. However, every small to mid-level agency does that. So, what can we do to separate ourselves gentleman?" He answers his own question without waiting for a response from the two men.

"We can prepare our clients for life after their chosen sports careers! Whether it's mutual fund investments, clubs, car lots, broadcasting or even motivational speaking...we owe it to our clients to equipment them with some life after their sports career skills," Vontez adamantly states to his cohorts. He continues, "If we truly want to live by the creed "my brother's keeper" we can't just look out for their financial interest while they're under contract with us. We have to treat them like family and make sure that the multitudes of money that they make during their playing careers, sustains them for their lifetime, and possibly for generations to come."

Bernard and Louis were moved by Vontez's stirring arguments on the behalf of current and future clients. The three men discussed the new focus of their company and exchanged ideas of what ventures would benefit the current Clientele roster. It was agreed that from that day forward, the sports agency known as "My Brother's Keeper" would truly live up to their name.

Meanwhile...........

"Shhhh, don't wake the kids, I just laid them down for their nap," Regina says in a demure fashion, as Verdale makes sexual advances at his attractive spouse.

Holding her waist and grinding on her firm round ass while standing behind her, Verdale softly kisses his wife on the nape of her neck, sending shockwaves of pleasure shuddering down her ample body. Moving his hand downward to grasp her curvaceous hips, his kisses leave a trail of tingles from her neck to her exposed shoulder. Gentle cries of desire escape Regina's pouty lips as they look back out of their children's bedroom, gingerly closing the door and being careful not to awaken them.

Once in the seclusion of the hallway, she lifts her arms in the air instinctively, allowing Verdale to remove her off-the-shoulder halter to top, exposing her firm 34C breast with larger than average nipples. Verdale spins his alluring partner around ravenously lock lips with her. She gracefully jumps up to mount him, wrapping her voluptuous thighs and legs around his slender waist. He carries her to the end of the hall entering into their massive master bedroom. Verdale lays her down on their bed and while releasing his hold on her, finds the waist band of her yoga pants and relieves her lower-half of her garment.

Already shirtless, and his manhood standing rock-hard in his boxers, Verdale takes them off uncovering his well-endowed penis. He pauses seductively, gazing with animal lust into his wife's eyes before lowering his head to kiss her hardened nipples. He tenderly kisses her right breast, while he sensually caresses her left, sending his wife into a daze of excitement dampness of her vulva with his thumb, leaving his wife arching her back from the sensation.

Minimum words had been spoken, but bounds of messages had been sent. Although married for over. He repeats his method of passion, kissing her left breast and caressing the right one, giving her body equal opportunity at pleasure. His kisses trail downward past her bellybutton and the sweet aroma of her warm wet pussy tickle the sense of Verdale's nostrils. He spreads her legs and softly strokes the

5 years, these two people were still as madly in love with one another as they had been when they first plummeted into deep depths of affection. Verdale starts to lick his wife's skillfully manicured pussy from the bottom (the space between her asshole and pussy) to the clitoris, like a cat licking a bowl of warm milk. He licks and sucks, sucks and nibbles every crevice of the womb of the woman he loved. The woman who bore his offspring; the woman who he was loyal to. He orally pleasured his woman until she begged for him to make love to her.

Lifting his head from her cum soaked *"love cave"*, Verdale's wet face met his lovers. She kissed and licked off the sweet, sticky juices from his face. He carefully plunged his dick inside of her, sending his wife into a murmur of moans and groans from the intense joy and delight of her man being inside of her. The couple makes love repeatedly that afternoon, reaffirming and solidifying something that they both already knew. They were soulmates, kindred spirits and most importantly, unmistakably in-love.

Chapter 6

Tae and Lil Dee were brothers who were two years apart in age. Tae was 28 and Lil Dee was 26. The brothers had ambitiously worked their way up the *"hustlin ladder"* as a part of the team of go-getters that Vontez had assembled over his years in the game. Snake's voluntary departure left a hole in the team's armor that the two brothers opportunistically filled. Vontez peeped the hunger in both of the brothers when they were young *"weed boys"* on his side of town. Men more than twice their age were copping from the brothers. Although they shared the same mother, but different fathers, both men were natural born *"hustlas"*. Both were charming young men that people loved to be around, males and females alike. Even though they were drastically different in appearance, Tae being 5'8", high-yellow, slim build with light brown eyes, and Lil Dee being 5'3", dark skinned and stocky with handsome chiseled features, they shared an unmistakable bond of love and loyalty for one another.

Growing up in the neighborhood of Westwood, you couldn't fight one without having to fight both of them. They easily made the transition from selling weed to coke during a weed drought one year. Vontez had called the young men over to his car one day as they chilled in the neighborhood park. Vontez had never spoken to the young men before, but his reputation preceded him because they absolutely knew who he was.

Vontez easily convinced the two brothers to try their hand at the lucrative cocaine business, under his tutelage of course. He let them know that his was more of a business expansion than a business departure. The brothers let their cousins, J-Ro and Keland, take over their weed *licks*, although they still made money off each transaction. When the weed drought was over, they used their people skills to see who was *copping "weight"* in their hood.

Pretty soon after their initial conversation with Tez, the two brothers had their ducks in a row. They told Vontez that they could handle about 12-16 ounces a week. Just like the boss he was, he gave them their first brick, knowing that they had underestimated their abilities as hustlas and the potency of his product. To their surprise, just like Vontez anticipated, the brothers sold out in three days. After that the two brothers, Tae and Lil Dee, were hooked and officially members of the "*Dope Game.*" That was over a decade ago when Tae was 17 and Lil Dee was around 15, and the two brothers became loyal family and key players on Tez's team.

Even after his incarceration, the brothers stepped up their game even more to fill the void that Snake left. They even sent pictures and letters to their friend and mentor when he was locked up. And just like true team players, they followed Verdale's leadership and instructions while their mentor in the game was away. Having family down south and cousins who were already coming to the city to "*get on*", they were in perfect position to make the transition and move to Atlanta.

After spending the weekend in Las Vegas enjoying the fight and post-fight activities, the siblings had taken a direct flight to Atlanta to kick it and tie up some loose ends in the city. The two men had recently purchased some properties, one being an above average sized 4 bedroom home, in the neighborhood of Buckhead in Atlanta. Both men were single and ready to mingle, and neither of them felt the need to get their own place at that time. The brothers had always shared everything and sharing women was no exception, because they were loyal to one another and pussy could never come between them. They took a cab to their crib from the airport, arriving there with plenty of daylight left in the day.

"Aye bruh, after we put these bags up why don't we call Red and see if he got the rest of that paper he owe down?" Tae remarks to his younger brother about one of their cousins in the city.

"I'll hit his ass up, but you already know that nigga either at Magic City or Strokers, with his *trickin* ass," Lil Dee responds.

"I swear that muthafucka would be rich right now if it wasn't for his *trick bill*!" Tae says empathically.

39

"You would think so with all the niggas in the game that he know! But it is what it is *Bruh Bruh*. The nigga always pay what he owe even if his motto is "trick first pay later", Dee says with a chuckle.

After putting away their belongings, Lil Dee makes the call and just like they expected, their cousin was headed to Strokers. Luckily, they caught him before he was in route and he agreed to bring the money he owed with him. The men had brought their two classic cars to the city of Atlanta when they brought their personal home. They had 71 Corvette Stingray and a 73 Chevy Caprice Classic on 26" rims.

"Let's take the Caprice since its got a back seat", expresses Tae.

"Bet, I'm driving", Lil Dee proclaims as he grabs the car keys off the key ring holder.

They arrive at Strokers in less than 30 minutes and Tae hits Red on his cell phone letting him know that they are in the parking lot.

"There he go", Lil Dee says to his brother after observing their cousin coming out of the strip club.

"Flash the lights", Tae commands.

Red acknowledges their presence with a head nod and he goes to his car to retrieve the 10 grand he owed his cousins out of his glove compartment, before getting in the backseat of the Caprice.

"What's good Fam? How was the fight?" Red asks his cousins with excitement in his voice.

"It was straight. Pacquiao should've let them hands go a lil more but it was a good fight doe," Lil Dee remarks as he gives his big cousin dap.

Tae turns around in the passenger seat to give Red dap too, and his cousin places an envelope containing the money in his hand. "What up doe Playboy?" Tae smiles as he makes the comment to his family member.

"Shit, you know what it is Fam-Fam. *Stayin* out these lame ass niggas way", Red replies and continues on to say,

"Hey, *muthafuckas* been getting shit lined up for when y'all ready to come down here on the regular. Ray, June-Bug and Jay-Gill have touched base with they folks in New Orleans, Albany and Tallahassee so we should be able to get rid of whatever y'all come *wit* quick, fast and in a hurry. That is, if that ticket is right?" Red says with a hint of sarcasm that the brothers peeped immediately.

"Don't worry "thirst magnet", it's gonna be some room on this ticket for you to make some more trick money!" Tae mockingly states to Red.

The three men partake in light-hearted laughter at the truthfulness of the statement. Red was spoiled and although he hustled and new a lot of niggas in the game, he didn't have to grind to shine like most cats who got down. His parents were well off so he didn't mind *jackin* off wads of cash on broads. Lil Dee twisted up a blunt of some blueberry Kush, and they smoked and chopped it up in the parking lot before they left to go home, and Red returned back into the strip club.

Back in Cinti..........

Lil Eric had grown increasingly curious to his father's whereabouts. Samantha hadn't mustered up the courage to tell him that his father had been shot, and was in jail. She told him that his daddy was away on business. With new developments in his case, there was more than just a ray of light at the end of the tunnel. Their hot shot attorney, Harvey Weinstein, had all but assured her that her husband would be back in her arms by the end of the summer. With only a little less than a month left in the school year, she was already making plans for Eric Jr. to go away for summer camp to keep his mind off of his father's absence.

She had to let him speak to his father in short stints on the phone so they could avoid the recording informing them that the phone call was being recorded and monitored by the federal authorities. Samantha didn't like to lie to her son, but her elusiveness from the truth was very necessary to keep her son's childhood innocence intact. She pulled up in front of the school around the yellow buses that lined the school's front circle to pick up a smiling Eric Jr., standing in his school uniform with a backpack in hand.

"Hey lil man! How was school today?" Samantha says with a big motherly smile on her face as her son enters the car and closes the door behind him.

"It was fun! I had art class today and we made family pictures with paint!" the excited 7 year old responds to his mother.

"I can tell. I thought y'all was supposed to wear aprons when y'all paint?" Samantha retorts while looking at the rainbow of colors on the top of her son's shirt.

"I did have one on, but I still got some on my shirt. I'm sorry mommy," the sincere youngster says appealing to his mother's soft-side.

"It's alright baby, just be more careful next time".

"My picture turned out good mommy! I can't wait for you to see it!"

"Where is it?" she asked.

"I had to let it dry first. It's a picture of you and daddy, and me and a dog, and a baby brother."

"A baby brother! What made you do that?" a surprised Samantha asks her son.

"I want a little brother to teach stuff to like some of my friends in class. Can you and daddy have a baby mommy?"

His purity was refreshing and Samantha simply answered "Ask *yo* daddy tonight when he calls okay?"

"O.k. momma."

"You want some McDonald's E.J.?"

"Yay, some chicken nuggets!"

And with that they were headed to the nearest "Mickey D's" with Samantha pondering the thought of having another child with E-Tone. It was a definite possibility because once she had her man back in her arms, there was no way she was letting him out of her sight.

Chapter 7

A week had passed since Luke had been shot and killed the "Snake Pit". It was truly a somber time in the lives of all who knew him. Luke's kindness, loyalty and humorous personality were infectious traits that had earned him scores of friends and associates. His parents and children were taking it particularly hard. Luke was an only child, who was the pride and joy of his parent's life, who had been married for over 30 years. Being the only child, Luke was always spoiled by his hardworking parents. His father was a foreman at a General Motors plant, and his mother was a nurse at Mercy South in Louisville. He also had excelled in sports, which enabled him to receive a scholarship to the University of Louisville, where he met and played football with Tiny before an ankle injury that ended his dreams of making it to the "Pros".

Luke was entering the prime of his life, at the age of 29, when he was gunned down. Along with being a bouncer at the club, Luke was more than active in his 6 and 7 year old son's lives. He was the coach of their Pee-wee football teams, and a father figure role model to the other young men that the coached. Although they were no longer together, Shanna, his baby mama, appreciated and admired how he always made time for his two boys. A role that "Uncle Tiny" was more than willing to now fill. He and Luke had played 3 years together on the defensive line at U of L, before Tiny had played 6yrs in the CFL and Arena Football leagues, before giving up on his passion due to back problems.

Tiny was in a state of depression and shock since the loss of his best friend. He had never had to deal with the death of someone that he was this close to before. Tiny, along with Virgil, Chubbs, Snake, Jerome and one of Luke's cousins, Daniel, were the designated pallbearers for the funeral ceremony. Even though Luke's parents were well-off and could easily afford to pay for the funeral expenses, especially since they still had an insurance policy on him, Snake wouldn't allow them to pay for anything concerning the funeral services. A sense of guilt has consumed him, since the night Luke was killed. He tried to rationalize mentally that it wasn't his fault; that there was nothing that he could do to change the hand of cards that fate had unmistakably dealt. But in his heart, he felt responsible for all who worked at his establishment. He considers everyone there as a part of his extended family.

Snake employed the services from the most respected funeral home in Louisville, "Final Resting Place Funeral Home", to preside over Luke's home going services. The wake and funeral were being held at Luke's family church, First Baptist

Church of Louisville. Reverend Alvin Jackson was the senior pastor of the church and would be delivering the Eulogy and sermon. He was also deeply saddened, as was everyone who knew Luke, because he had watched the young man grow up from a mischievous young boy to a responsible adult; one who brought his own children to the same church that had nurtured his spirit as a youth.

It was a dreary Saturday morning. Dark ominous clouds decorated the sky, as droves of funeral parishioners formed a line extending down the steps of the church to pay their respects to Luke. Cries, sobbing, and weeping could be heard outside, coming from the front of the church as grieving friends and family viewed the body. Those who hadn't totally broken down as they took their final gaze at Luke's lifeless corpse, gave their heartfelt condolences to his parents, baby mama, and children, who were seated in the front row. Former teammates, ex-girlfriends, childhood classmates, mothers and fathers of the young men whom he had coached (and some of the children), and a host of other friends and family filled the pews of the church.

The church organist had been softly playing church hymns as the viewers viewed the body and took their seats. Some were crying, while others tried to comfort and console them. Some were reading the obituary, while others were hugging and greeting old friends, acquaintances and teammates they hadn't seen in many years. The church was packed full of mourners, and the choir came from behind the church stage to fill the choir sections of the stage. The pastor followed after them, taking a seat in his throne-like plush chair, positioned 6 feet directly behind the podium. The organist finished the hymn he was playing as the line of people viewing the impacted the lives of all who knew and loved this young man. But the answer is that it's simply a part of God's plan body slowly dissipated.

The choir stood as the organist began playing "Precious Lord". The lead vocalist sang a stirring rendition of the song, bringing those who were teetering on the brink of tears to full-blown balling. Once the somber song was finished, the pastor stood and announced that the reading of the obituary would be read by the best friend of the dearly departed, Henry "Tiny" Rhodes. Tiny sorrowfully read the obituary, getting more and more choked up with each sentence that he completed until he was finished and in tears. Precious stood up to comfort him halfway through the reading, patting and rubbing on his back until he completed the dreary task. After Tiny and Precious were seated, the pastor stood up and solemnly strolled up to the pulpit.

Pastor Jackson began, "The Bible shows as we have seen, that God has a plan for everything. God planned

everything before the world began. He had a plan for Adam and Eve, a plan for faithful families from Noah to

Jacob; God had a plan for the nation of Israel from Moses to the exile and beyond. He had a plan for the prophets and a plan for his Son Jesus. He has a plan for the church and a plan to bless those who choose to believe in his son. He also has a plan for the future. Events yet to happen on this planet are all a part of His plans.....And so, we have to be careful when we say that someone has died an untimely death.

48

We are all deeply saddened and we have heavy hearts because of the unfortunate circumstances that surround the departure of our beloved Luke. It was a senseless and unnecessary turn of events that leaves us to ask the question "why"? Why would God allow this tragedy to happen? I know that the answer may not sit well with some of you right now because the pain of this loss is so great. I know that the answer may not give some of you the comfort that you seek at this time because you are trying to make sense of this devastating event that has.

The bible says in Proverbs 3:5, *"Trust in the Lord with all your heart and lean not on your own understanding."* Now, is one of those times when God's plan is beyond our own earthly comprehension. God's plan is not confined to what we would have happen. God's plan is not restricted to the desires of our heart. God's plan is not limited by our own timeline. And because he is God, for those of us who trust and believe in His word, we have to believe that when things happen, good or bad, that it's all according to His divine purpose and plan. Can I get an Amen somebody? So again, I say that you have to be careful when you use the phrase "he died an untimely death", simply because we are on God's schedule and God doesn't make mistakes.

One thing that gives me comfort in the particular case, is I don't have to ask the question, was this brother saved? I don't have to wonder if this young man had accepted Jesus Christ as his Lord and Savior. I don't have to speculate as to whether or not this young man was right with God, because I fellowshipped with this brother on a weekly basis. And so, as I have found comfort in knowing that, I urge the family and friends of Luke to also find solace in that fact. And just like this young man was a great example in life, let's not let his death be in vain. By a show of hands, how many of you young men and women under the sound of my voice are saved? By a show of hands..... (Less than half of the mourners raised their hands. The majority being the church members who had come to pay respects). And because we know that God's plan and our earthly plans may not be in alignment, you want to be right with God no matter when the "angel of death" appears. You'll be ready! Can I get an Amen! (And the stirring crowd responds with an Amen!) Let us not focus on how this young man died, but more importantly on how he lived his life! And this young man, although he wasn't perfect because we all fall short of the glory of God, he was saved and he was ready. Can I get an Amen! The Bible teaches us that God will come back like a thief in the night, and it doesn't literally mean at night time. It means that no one knows when the hour of death is upon you. So in turn, you have to be ready." The words of the preacher were rousing the "Holy Spirit" in the room, and the hardened hearts of many were softening like hard soil on a rainy day.

Snake was particularly feeling the Holy Spirit. Whether it was guilt from his past transgressions, or if it was the guilt of Luke's death, that was messing with his conscience. He began to feel an overwhelming feeling of emotion. The more Rev. Jackson preached his message of salvation, the more Snake felt the urge to give his life to Christ. Rev. Jackson continued, "One thing I want you to know about giving your life to Christ is that once you do, you're a new person. You have a fresh start when you're born again and you'll see life through a different set of eyes. The sins of your past won't be held against you once you accept Jesus Christ as your Lord and Savior. The Bible says in 2 Corinthians 5:17, "Therefore, if anyone is in Christ, he is a new creation, old things have passed away. Behold, all things have become new.""

Rev. Jackson preached a beautiful heartfelt message of salvation that Saturday morning, even having an altar-call before the end of the funeral ceremony. Five mourners, including Snake, made their way down the aisle to hold hands and repeat these words after Rev. Jackson, "Dear Heavenly Father, I repent of my sins. I believe that your son, Jesus Christ, died on the cross for my sins and I accept Him as my Lord and Savior. I ask that You come into my life to make me whole."

After repeating those words after the preacher, Snake felt a feeling of relief. Like a ton of bricks had been lifted off his shoulders. Candy was smiling through her tears as Snake walked back to his seat in the church. She greeted him with open arms, hugging him tightly and telling him how proud she was of him and how much she loved him. Tears were rolling down his face but he didn't feel ashamed. The tears acted like a "rinse cycle" washing away the many sins that had haunted his soul. Snake continued to hug and embrace the other members of his extended family from the club, including his real cousin, Jerome, and his sisters Juanita, and Joyce. They were all so proud of him at that moment, as were the families of the other mourners who had chosen to give their lives to Christ as well.

The reverend wrapped up the service calling for the pallbearers to step forward to carry the casket. As they emerged from the church, the dreary skies turned into clear skies as if Luke was giving them one final sign that he was totally at peace. The mourning turned into a celebration of Luke's life, just like he would have wanted. The enormous funeral procession flowed through the streets of Louisville to the cemetery where Luke's body would forever rest. Afterwards, everyone attended the repast that was held at a banquet hall that Snake rented and catered. Stories of Luke's escapades and antics had everyone's spirits lifted. Memories of Luke continued to entertain in his death as they did during his life.

Chapter 8

It was Sunday, mid-morning, and Vontez, Stephanie, and Keisha had just awoken from another lust-filled night of pleasure. The ladies promptly showered together, washing each other's backs as they had done on so many occasions before. Vontez slipped on some shorts and went downstairs to prepare brunch for them while they showered and styled each other's hair before getting dressed. His phone rings, and he immediately notices the "740" area code that graced the phone's screen. He answered knowing that it was his homeboy, Daryl, calling from the joint.

"This phone call originates from an Ohio Correctional Facility. All conversations will be recorded and monitored. To accept this phone call please press zero, to reject please press nine," the voice recording on the other end of the phone says. Vontez presses zero to accept the phone call.

"What's up D? What's good *wit ya* homie?" Vontez says happy to hear his friend's voice.

"Tez! I'm *chillin, chillin*. What you up to out there?" Daryl asks his friend with genuine excitement in his voice.

"Man, you know me better than anybody D! I'm *stickin* to the script. *Stayin* focused out this *muthafucka*! *Bout* to make some steak and eggs for me and my ladies before we get our day started," Vontez informs Daryl.

"That sounds good as fuck right now! I ain't had no steak in damn near 6 years. I can't wait to get out this *muthafucka*! Another 20 months and I should be in the halfway house. You know they automatically giving out T.C. (Transitional Control) if you doing more than 2yrs!" Daryl says forgetting if Vontez was still in prison when the new law had passed.

"Yeah I remember them saying that. They should have been took that decision out of the judges hands. Them dickheads from our city was barely giving that shit out. You still been *hittin that bar*?" Vontez poses the question.

"You already know! Remember Germaine out of Columbus?"

"Yeah"! exclaims Vontez.

"He been *gettin it in* with me", Darryl says in a hyped tone.

"That's what's up! What's up *wit* ole girl, Lisa? Is she still *ridin wit* you?" Vontez inquires.

"Hell yeah! She a thoroughbred fo'real. Matter of fact, she got a visit scheduled in two weeks on the 24th", a lucky and confident Daryl replies.

"Okay then, that's what's up. I dropped some money off to your moms. Did you get it?" asked Vontez.

"Yeah I did Tez, I really appreciate that my nigga."

"No problem Bruh, Bruh! You know I got you!"

"I'm salty I didn't get to see the big fight. I heard it was one for the ages!" Darryl says with disappointment.

"Yeah it was! Ain't nobody gonna beat that boy "Money Mayweather"! His defense is too slick!" Vontez says acknowledging Mayweather's skills.

"You ain't never lied about that shit! That boy is slick!" Daryl retorts.

"What's up with Turtle? Have you heard from him again?" an inquisitive Vontez asks.

"Yeah, he wrote me about a week ago. He's doing alright. He told me that he got into the dental program up there so he gets 5 good days a month. Shit, he'll knock 2 months off the 2 years he got!" Daryl declares with joy for his younger brother.

"Hell yeah, that's what's up! I'm glad to hear that for him. What about you? Are you still running those programs?" Vontez directs the question to his homeboy.

"The only one I'm teaching now is a program I developed called MSM (Man Sharpening Man). It's a program to teach these young cats who come through the system the principles of manhood. With all the daddies and father figures they have locked up, it's no wonder that half of these lil niggas act like bitches! I figured it was time to give back a little. You know, help polish these young cats up. I was thinking about bringing this shit to the streets on some non-profit organization type shit!" Daryl tells Vontez.

"That's some good shit D! Them lil niggas need that fo'real. I could help you set that up once you get home with no problem. If that's what you wanna do?" Vontez declares to him.

"I appreciate that Bruh, Bruh. I wanna see how this first class goes, but yeah, I think that sounds like a plan right there. I didn't want shit this morning Tez, just checking on you. They about to close the dayroom for count, so I'm gon let you go back to cooking for your "wonder twins", and I'll hit you back next week," announces Daryl.

"Bet homie, take care of yourself and I'll holla at you!" Vontez says before ending the phone call.

Vontez continued to make brunch with positive thoughts swirling around in his head, as he thought about Daryl's plans. He reflected on the remarkable strides of growth and maturity that Daryl had made since he had gotten locked up damn near 6 years ago. Vontez was looking forward to helping his loyal friend transition into the positive role model that he inadvertently was becoming.

Meanwhile........

Mama V had awoken that morning, distraught from her dream from the night before. It was about Verdale again, and the 4th dream she'd had about him in the last few months. She went into the kitchen and made herself a cup of coffee to help calm her nerves but it was to no avail. She debated to herself if she should call him or not. She didn't want to spook him, but she had never been wrong about her dreams before. When she previously had dreams, the events or persons she dreamt about had come to fruition within a month or so but this time it was different. She had already shared the content of one of her dreams with him and that in itself made her uncomfortable, but the guilt of not revealing her dreams to Vontez and their father had taken a toll on her mentally. She just had to talk to somebody so she decided to call her sister-in-law, Margret. The phone rang a couple of times before Margret answered.

"Hey girl! How are you this fine Sunday morning?" Margaret greeted her sister-in-law thru the phone.

"Good Morning Margy. Girl I had another one of those dreams again, and girl it's got me all flustered this morning," Mama V reports.

"Was it about Dale again?"

"Yes it was and now I'm really worried something awful *bout* him!" Mama V says with serious concern in her voice.

"Well V, all you can do is pray about it. The Lord is the only one who knows for sure what the future holds for that boy, so you can't stress yourself about it sis. You coming to church this morning?" Margaret asked of her worrying sister-in-law.

"Yes, I'll be there. And I know you're right, God has the steering wheel, and I just pray that he directs my baby boy's path."

"He will V, He will. Was it the same dream as the last time or something different?" Margret inquires.

"It was about rats again, but this time it was a giant rat following him but he couldn't see it. Every move he made, every place he went the rat was trailing close behind, but Verdale couldn't see him or didn't even notice him for that matter! But you right Margy, I told him to watch his back and be careful. All I can do now is pray on it," Mama V's saddening voice trailed off.

"Well like I said I don't want you to worry yourself to death about it. It's in the Lords hands now. I'll see you in church about 10:30 ok?"

"Ok girl" Mama V says before hanging up the phone.

She knew that it was out of her hands and prayer was the only thing that could give her comfort now. Mama V got herself together after she finished her cup of coffee and smoked half a blunt before hopping in the shower. As the streams of water beat against her naked back, Valencia prayed that her baby boy be covered in the "blood of Jesus" for his sake and hers. She didn't know if her heart could take another tragedy in her life.

Chapter 9

"I can't believe that I'm going to be playing in the NFL! And to top it off, I'm not going to be that far away from home Ma! Maryland is only a few hours away from Charlotte," Logan comments to his loving Mother.

"I'm so proud of you Son! All of your hard work is paying off, just like I knew it would! And just think, when your Daddy first signed you up for the PeeWee league, I was terrified that you would get hurt!" his Mother Tricia, honestly states to her Son.

"Yea, she was so overprotective of you son! I had to promise her that if you got hurt once, that I would pull you off the team. But I knew you were built for that game. I had been chasing and play tackling you since you could walk...and you would just be laughing and running and just instinctively joking and shaking me like a running back! Man, it was something to see! You're a natural Son, and I couldn't be more proud of you too!" Lorenzo says, gleaming with pride to his Son.

"It still hasn't completely hit me yet. Even when the phone call from the coach, and then hearing the Commissioner say, *"With the 55th pick in the 2015 NFL draft, the Baltimore Ravens selected Logan Williams from Wake Forest University!"* It was surreal!" Logan remarks with all smiles.

"Well, I think you made a good choice going with MBK Sports Agency. It seems like they will go the extra mile for you Son. With them sending a limousine to take you to the airport, it seems like they're giving you the royal treatment," remarks Logan's Mother.

"I'm sure that your agents are going to talk to you about how there's more to being a professional football player, and not just playing football. You have to carry yourself with respect and integrity. It's not because you're better than anybody else, but because you are going to be held to a higher standard. Everything that you do will be judged under a microscope. Everything you do will be scrutinized. Something as simple as a routine traffic stop will be news worthy, simply because of who you are! You hear me Son?" Lorenzo exclaims to his Son.

"Yes Sir! I totally understand Dad!" Logan responds.

"And, with the racial climate in this country and especially with the recent events in Baltimore, you have a real chance to make a positive impact on that community," Lorenzo continues to say to his Son. It's a damn shame what happened to that young man, Freddy Gray! Just a damn shame! I don't know what's going on with these police officers nowadays. TreVaughn Martin, Michael Brown, Eric Gardner, the young man in Cleveland, the man in South Carolina...the list goes on and on."

"And, the bottom line is that they were all senseless killings!" Tricia chimes in passionately about the topic.

"I'll tell you what's wrong with them...it's because they're scared of our young men, plain and simple! They're scared of 'em because they haven't been raised around black folks, and they only believe what they see on the news, or rap videos about us! And on top of that, most of the young white cops were bullied in high school or had some other issues. And then they get a little bit of authority and a gun! That's a volatile mix for sure!" exclaims Lorenzo.

"I know that's right Renzo! But let's not put a damper on this joyous occasion. After all, Logan is going there to negotiate his contract, visit with the team owners and view the facilities. Let's not fill his head with all of our social consciousness views. Baby you go down there and just be you and you'll be fine!" Tricia says as she pinches her Son's cheeks.

"Yea, you're mama's right. Go down there and make the team first and then change the world!" Lorenzo chuckles and pats his Son on the back.

"I am! Plus, Bernard and Louis have already mentioned to me about being active in the city of Baltimore. There is a lot of rebuilding going on in the city, and I want to be apart of the solution in the city. After all, I do have a degree in political science. I think it will come in handy if I am asked some questions by the local media about what's going on down there," Logan comments to his loving and concerned parents before the doorbell rings. 'That must be my ride!" Logan blurts out.

"You have a safe trip Baby and be sure to call us once you get settled...You hear me?" Tricia says with motherly concern.

"Yeah, it's your ride! I'll help you with your bags," Lorenzo yells from the living room after answering the door.

Logan said his goodbyes to his parents to begin a journey that he had worked so hard to achieve his entire life. He felt even better to be meeting his agents, Louis and Bernard, in Baltimore, to be his guide through the process that was ahead. He was feeling more than thankful, he was feeling truly blessed.

Chapter 10

It was the afternoon of Friday, May 29. Precious, Monique, and Fawn were all working behind the bar, stocking up liquor and slicing lemons and limes for drink garnishments. Tiny was bringing liquor and beer from the basement stockroom, and Chubbs was cleaning the restrooms. Luke's joking and playful presence was obviously missed around the club. The lack of his magnetic personality was apparent, due to the absence of laughter in the atmosphere. It had been nearly a month since the tragedy at the club. The crowd had fallen off for a couple of weeks, because of the violent occurrence, but now that the detectives who were assigned to the murders had captured the perpetrator, they were hoping that business would pick up.

The theme for this evening was a "Grown and Sexy" happy hour. Jerome hired a local band that played R & B and jazz, to create the ambiance for the club that evening.

Customers had yet to arrive, but the happy hour wasn't scheduled to begin for a couple of hours.

"Lawd have mercy! It sho' is some nasty ass folks in the world!" Chubbs bellows out, as he exits the men's restroom.

"It seems like most men can't control their "thing", even when they want to! Always pissin' on the toilet seat and the floor," Monique says with disgust.

Precious chimes in, "Girl, you ain't never lied! I'm always cussin' my baby daddy out about pissin' on the toilet seat. He says it happens when he shakes it."

"I don't know which is worse, a pissy toilet seat or a pissy dick!" Fawn says, and the ladies laugh.

"Girl, it's got to be a pissy dick! Ain't nothin' like gittin' ready to give yo man some head and his dick smell like a pissy pamper! *Talkin bout* a mood killer!' Monique adds to the conversation, and the ladies continue to erupt in laughter.

"It's good to hear y'all laughing again...Luke wouldn't have wanted y'all to stay sad for so long," Tiny says as he comes from downstairs with a case of Bud Light.

"Yeah! You're right Tiny! Luke always tried to keep a smile on everybody's face...seems only right that we joke more if nothing else but to honor his memory!" Precious states to the others.

"Well I'm all for that!" Chubbs chimes in. "I knew you sucked dick Monique...I could tell by how you suck the sauce off them chicken wings before you eat '*me*," he says, telling the first raunchy joke as the group explodes in laughter.

"Oh, no you didn't! With your fat ass! You need to take a pregnancy test with that big ole belly of yours!" You gotta be at least 4 months! Monique fires back.

The group continues to bombard each other with harmless obscene jokes, until the band arrives to set up their equipment. It was the first time they were able to move past their grief as a group. And they had to admit to each other that it felt good to be able to celebrate the spirit of Luke in that fashion.

When Snake and Candy arrived, they could tell that their staff was returning back to normal. Tiny and Chubbs had the ladies in an all-out laughing frenzy, when they walked in with their competing imitation of Rick Ross. They were matching each other grunt for grunt. Snake and Candy joined in the goof-off with the other bar staff. It had been weeks since Snake had even felt like joking. Since his spiritual conversion, he had let Jerome move all of the "*werk*" he had left, and told him once he moved the 34 bricks, that he would turn him on to a *plug*. Jerome had been wanting his chance in the limelight and with Sapphire due in a little over a month, he was eager to collect some extra dividends.

The band, "Urban Experience", arrived with an hour to spare before happy hour was due to start at 5 pm. They were setting up when Joyce, Calvin, Juanita and Larry came in to get drinks before opening up the food truck at 6 pm.

"Hey, what's up cut?! How is everybody doing?" Joyce says first since she was the person in front of their small group.

The rest followed with their hellos and greetings. They couldn't help but notice the jovial energy in the room; the first they had experienced since before the tragic fight night.

"Hey, has anybody talked to Rome or Sapphire today? They should be here by now," Juanita exhorts.

"I did talk to him this morning...but let me try him now," Snake says as he pulls out his cellphone to make the call. He makes three attempts to call his cousin, with no luck. "That's odd, he's not answering," says Snake with slight concern.

"He's probably tied up! You know him and Sapphire can't keep their hands off each other!" adds Candy.

"You know that's right!" Joyce blurts out signifying her agreement with Candy.

"Whose idea was it to have the band? I heard these cats play before. They live as hell!" Calvin remarks trying to change the conversation.

"It was Jerome's idea," Snake says while still trying to call him again, but getting the same results.

He was slightly worried, because if Jerome didn't answer his phone (which was a rarity), he would always call right back. The band begins to warm up, playing the Frankie Beverly and Maze classic, "Golden Time of Day." The collection of people in the bar turned their attention to the stage where the band was set up, admiring the soothing sounds that exuded from the speaker system. There was an instant calm that came over the crowd as the music of Frankie Beverly and Maze often does to its listeners.

Although Snake was still perplexed as to why Jerome hadn't returned his call, he dismissed it as his cousin being caught up with Sapphire. The group laughed and danced while the band played on. They drank the bar's signature drink – "Snake Venom" (a vodka mixed with cranberry, pineapple, and orange juice with a splash of Grenadine) and took shots of "Grey Goose," while enjoying each other's company until the "30 and Over" happy hour crowd they were anticipating arrived.

Chapter 11

Fernando "Flash" Alverez was short in stature, but big in bravado. He stood at a modest 5'7", 160 lbs., but had the "swag" of a man twice his size. Whether it was a "Napoleon Complex" he possessed or just his fiery Latino blood, Flash was living proof of the phrase, it's not the size of the dog in the fight, but the size of the fight in the dog!" His beautiful wife, Sophia, was a "dead ringer" for the Latina bombshell, Eva Longoria. They had met at a yacht party thrown by the leader of the "Intrepido Guerrero" Cartel (meaning "Fearless Warrior"), Rafael Marco, five years ago; and the flashy ladies' man was smitten at first sight.

Sophia, being the niece of Rafael, had been spoiled her entire life. Her father, Roberto, Rafael's brother had been killed by a rival cartel when she was just a baby. Her mother, who was a young servant girl, was in no position to raise her, so her uncle Rafael raised her as his own. At the time they had met, Flash had climbed the ranks to become a lieutenant on his own merits because of the ruthlessness and advantageous conduct on the cartel's behalf. Since the wedding and birth of their first child, Lucinda, Rafael had promoted Flash to a captain, although he didn't much care for his flashy behavior. Besides the business arrangements he had with the brothers in Ohio, Flash had two other major lines of distribution; one in Texas and the other in New York. With the new expansion deal, with the brothers from Ohio, he would be solely responsible for a thousand kilos of pure "Columbian cocaine" being moved monthly throughout the United States. He was indispensable to the organization.

Flash and Sophia, along with their two children, Lucinda (age 4) and Pedro (age 3), lived on a 10-acre ranch, with a mansion-style fortress, equipped with guards, and all to boot, in a secluded area of San Bernadino, CA. Once he became a Captain, his now uncle and boss, had told him to tone down his flamboyancy, due to safety concerns because of his new status in the cartel. Flash obliged while local, but when he held his business meetings in Las Vegas, he would let his *"nuts hang"*! Las Vegas, being a city known for its glitz, glamour and high rollers, was the perfect meeting destination for him......a place where his ostentatious displays of wealth would blend in with the rest of the gaudy tourists, and residents of the *"sin city."* He looked forward to his business encounters in the city that never sleeps, just to be able to spread his flashy wings.

Verdale and Vontez had contacted him about discussing "business," so he was looking forward to his meeting with the two brothers from Ohio. When he arrived in Vegas, via his private jet, the exotic rental company that he had a stellar relationship with had three high-end vehicles for him to choose from, at his request of course. The first was a bright red Bugatti, a silver Aston Martin, and a black Ferrari. He chose the Aston Martin, simply because he hadn't driven one yet.

He arrived a week early because he wanted to kill two birds with one stone; to meet his distributor from New York, and the two brothers from Ohio. Flash and the New York distributor met to discuss something that perturbed and perplexed him, once the topic revealed itself; the Cuban jobber, Rodolfo Cardona, wanted to sell guns to the cartel. Unbeknownst to Flash, this man was also an arms dealer. He had only been dealing with Rodolfo since taking over for his predecessor as Captain. Rodolfo informed Flash that he had access to military grade weapons and would be willing to trade weapons for product. The proposal had taken Flash by surprise. He let the New York merchant know that he would give it some thought and get back with him.

After the rendezvous with Rodolfo, Flash had a few days to unwind before his next meeting with Verdale and Vontez. But, he couldn't shake the uneasy feeling he had about his meeting with the New Yorker; numerous questions cluttered his mind. Had his predecessor done his homework on Rodolfo? What else was he involved in? Who else was he involved with?

Chapter 12

Vontez and Verdale were satisfied with the agreed upon deal they had worked out with Flash. The price of $10,500 per kilo was what they considered to be fair. The next shipment in July would be the first of many of the highly anticipated expansion. Verdale had leased a warehouse in the industrial district in Atlanta, in a Limited Liability Corporation (LLC) name. This was done to distance himself and his brother from any legal ties to the building, and to also add legitimacy to the paperwork, as they had done with the other drug hubs. Vontez and Verdale had set up a meeting with their understudies, Tae and Lil Dee, to work out the minor details of the out-of-town operations.

They met during the day, at a club called "The Grove", in a private V.I.P. room. The club was owned by an associate of Vontez, so their privacy wasn't an issue. The Lewis brothers were already seated at a table, in the VIP room, when Tae and Lil Dee arrived. They greeted each other with handshakes and brotherly hugs before they sat down to discuss the particulars of the avocation ahead of them.

Vontez starts the conversation by saying "what's good with y'all young playas?"

"Chilin', chilling' O.G." Tae responds.

"Ready to get this paper!" Lil Dee adds.

"I know that's right!" Verdale chimes in.

"OK den, well the warehouse is already taken care of, so the semi-truck will have a place to unload the product. Did y'all take care of the two stash houses, like I told y'all to?" Vontez questions the two siblings.

"Yeah, we closed on them last month. We got one in College Park and one in Lithonia," Tae says with admiration, to his mentor in the game.

"And we got our personal contractor, "Uncle T", to build a false wall in each of the basements, like you instructed!" Lil Dee verbalizes and waits for the brothers' approval.

"That's what's up Lil Niggas. I see y'all really been on y'all shit. But of course, I expect nothing less. After all, y'all have been groomed by the best!" Vontez tells the young men as he pops a bottle of very expensive champagne and fills up four glasses.

"What about y'all security? The systems and y'all personnel?" Verdale asked, trying to cover all the bases.

"We got our loyal "goons" making the move with us, so we're good as far as that's concerned," Lil Dee happily informs them.

"And Uncle T wired up the security systems and they ring to smart phones that we both have, to notify us, instead of the boys......and we have motion-sensitive camera systems in place as well," Tae says confidently.

"And the last and most important question that we have to ask, do y'all have all y'all licks lined up? I already know the answer, but I need to hear the confirmation from y'all mouth," Vontez finally says.

"We got it covered O.G.!" Lil Dee answers first.

"Well yeah, we got it covered, but what's our ticket gonna be?" Tae answers and asks the question in the same breath.

"Young Tae, forever the business man! Y'all paying 28 grand right now, we gonna knock it down to 23 grand a piece. And of course, you already know the quality!" Vontez states.

"Bet! It's on O.G.!" an excited Tae blurts out.

"I want to propose a toast to gettin' this paper as a family! Loyalty is Royalty!" Vontez declares and the other men respond... "Loyalty is Royalty!"

Verdale gives each brother, Tae and Lil Dee, a burner phone with his burner number already programmed in them. The men finished the bottle of bubbly and parted ways that afternoon, anticipating the lucrative move that would begin next month. Vontez told the men to contact Verdale on his "burner," about any further business questions. He told them to contact him only for personal matters on his line. The men knew not to question his authority, and because they were loyal team players, they would gladly oblige.

Chapter 13

"Girl, I was scared as hell when I saw them niggas come through the front and back doors". It was straight out of a *gangster* movie scene. I put on a *helluva* actin job *though*. I was even thinking about switching sides again, until I remembered that they had the spot surrounded. I had Snake and the agent's hand "zip-tied"! They exchanged some words and the next thing I know, bullets were flying everywhere. It all just got out of hand, so fast. All I could do was duck for cover! It was bitter sweet though, because although I am in love with Snake, I didn't want to see E-Tone and J.J. shot up like that! After all, we did spend years together gettin' this money. But it was the only way that me and you could be happy. The only way that you and I could truly be free from their stronghold on us!" Candy explains to Sapphire.

"Don't beat yourself up about it girl! It was the only way! Them niggas would have had to get rid of us, we knew too much!" Sapphire says to comfort Candy.

"Girl, but what really got me shook, is when E-Tone opened his eyes on that stretcher! He looked directly at me. And if you could have seen the look of surprise and hatred he had in his eyes for me! Well, I could have and would have died if looks could kill!" Candy recalls to Sapphire.

"Well, them niggas is out of the picture now! J.J. is dead and gone! God rest his soul! And E-Tone ain't *neva gon* see the light of day again. So now we can focus on being happy for once in our lives. God works in mysterious ways. We were sent here to end somebody's life and they end up giving us a fresh start on ours. I just want to have my baby and finally have the family that I have always wanted with Jerome and his people. I just want to be happy!" Sapphire says with tears in her eyes.

Candy snaps out of her daze, as she was recalling a past conversation that she and her best friend had shared. It had been over a week since Jerome and Sapphire had gone missing. When they didn't show up that night at the club, for the "happy hour" and the band, and didn't answer or return any of the numerous phone calls from anyone, the next day Snake took it upon himself to go by their house. When he arrived, he found the front door unlocked, the house ransacked and blood stained, and Jerome's Mercedes was missing. Snake, immediately but carefully looked for the "*bricks*" he had left in Jerome's care. He couldn't find any sign of them so he called the police. The police, to everyone's worst fears, had confirmed that the blood belonged to both Sapphire and Jerome. "Missing Posters" had been printed and placed throughout the city.

The "missing couple" was the headline story on all their local television stations, and the story had also received regional media coverage. Jerome's family was distraught. What happened to their beloved son and his pregnant wife was the obvious tear-jerking question that they were asking. Snake was feeling even more guilt than he felt about what happened to Luke. He wished he could get his hands on Jerome's phone to see who the last person was that called him, or who the last person was that Jerome called, before him and Sapphire went missing. But, the phone had to be missing or turned off because it was going straight to voicemail. Snake and the other family members were praying for the best, that they were still somehow alive. But Snake knew in his heart, that he should be prepared for the worst, that the chances of finding his cousin and his wife alive were slim to none.

It was Saturday, June 13th. It had been over two weeks now, since the couple went missing. Family and friends were losing hope at a rapid pace of ever seeing the couple alive again. Jerome's sisters, Joyce and Juanita, along with Candy, had organized a prayer vigil. It was being held on the steps of Ebenezer Baptist Church by Reverend Kenny Thompson, who was leading the prayer vigil. The family members were gathered around, as well as friends and supporters. Everyone held an unlit candle while standing in a circle.

Worship leader, Rev. Thompson begins, "I light this first candle as a symbolization as the light of hope! And as we light the other candles off of this candle, it is a symbolization of our hope growing together for the safe return of Brother Jerome and his loving wife, Sister Sapphire. Dear Heavenly Father Your word says in Romans 5 (1-5),

"Therefore having been justified by faith, we have peace with God through our Lord, Jesus Christ, through whom also we have access by faith into this grace in which we stand and rejoice in the hope and glory of God. And not only that, but we also glory in tribulations, knowing that tribulations produces perseverance, and perseverance produces character, and character produces hope. Now hope does not disappoint because the love of God has been poured out in our hearts by the Holy Spirit who was given to us".

Father we need you right now, Brother Jerome and Sister Sapphire need for you to intervene in their situation right now, Oh Lord! Father we know that your will, will be done! But we ask that you comfort Brother Jerome and Sister Sapphire while they are in the midst of this storm. Father we ask that you give comfort and peace to the family, Dear Lord, because they are hurting right now. They're hurting Father God, but they have faith in Your Word, Dear Lord! Your Word says in Hebrews 11:1, "Now faith is the substance of things hoped for the evidence of things not seen".

We are holding on to faith, Dear Lord. Father your Word says the answers to Your promises are "yes" and "Amen", so we will never question what Your will is in our life, Father God. We have faith that all things will work for the good to those who love God and those who are called according to His purpose. Father we just ask that you give comfort to this worried and grieving family, Dear Lord! Father your Word says in 2 Corinthians 3-4,

"Blessed be the God and the Father of our Lord Jesus Christ, the Father of mercies and God of all comfort, who comforts us in all our tribulations, that we may be able to comfort those who are in any trouble, with the comfort with which we ourselves are comforted by God."

Father we pray that you give us this comfort, we ask these things in Your Son's Jesus Christ name and the Body of Christ, say Amen!"

The people in attendance left that night feeling at peace that the situation was in God's hands. The next day the bodies were found bound and tied together in the Ohio River, badly decomposed and unrecognizable. They were identified through dental records. It wasn't the answer to their prayers that the family was hoping for, but at least they had some sense of closure. Although they didn't know "who" had committed the ghastly crime, Snake knew the "why". Jerome and Sapphire were tortured and murdered for the 34 bricks of cocaine that he had in his possession. But who did he tell? Who did he confide in with that information? That was the question that Snake was determined to find out.

Chapter 14

Tuesday, June 16th, was a beautiful day in more ways than one, for Eric "E-Tone" Carter. It was a sunny 80°F day with minimal clouds. It was an unofficial Black holiday, Tupac's birthday, and it was the day of his release. Harvey Weinstein, his savvy lawyer, was able to finagle his freedom by disclosing technicalities in the case. He left his cell for the last time, only taking the pictures of his family, and the letters his wife sent him. After signing release papers, he was handed a box and directed to enter the Men's restroom. Once inside he opened the box to reveal a letter addressed to him, a short-sleeved Polo shirt, some dark-blue Levi 501 jeans, a black belt, and a pair of size 10-1/2 all white Air Max shoes. Before getting dressed he opened and read the letter:

"Dear Mr. Carter, first off I want to congratulate you on your much deserved freedom. It was my pleasure making fools out of the Federal Prosecutors that handled your case. I look

forward to getting you monetary compensation for your wrongful conviction, although that will be a more lengthy process. Secondly, here are the items you requested. I am not much of a personal shopper, but I hope these items will suffice. And lastly, here is a plane ticket back to Ohio and $500 in cash, and also as you instructed, I didn't tell your wife, so you will be able to surprise her. I wish you luck and please get in contact with me in the next two weeks. Sincerely yours, Harvey Weinstein".

After reading the letter, E-Tone quickly got dressed and returned to the discharge area, where he handed the female officer his uniform, and she gave him a release I.D.

E-Tone was driven by a guard to the nearest airport, where he boarded a plane back to Cincinnati. After arriving at the Greater Cincinnati Airport, luggage free, E-Tone quickly hails a cab to his Suburban home. When he arrives, he sees his wife's silver Ford Explorer parked in the driveway. He gives the cab driver a $50 bill and tells the cab driver to keep the change before exiting the vehicle.

As *gangsta* as he was, E-Tone was beaming with child-like excitement, anticipating holding his sexy wife again. He debates to himself whether or not he should go around to the back patio door, but he rationalizes that as soon as his two pit bulls (a black male named Zeus, and a brindle female named Athena) saw him, they would bark like crazy, therefore spoiling his surprise arrival. He didn't want to enter the front door because of the door chimes and voice automation of the ADT security system. E-Tone took a more romantic and less startling, invasive approach. He picked a single red rose from the rose bush adjacent to his front door and rang the doorbell. He stood there with the innocence and apprehensiveness of a teenager going on a first date. Samantha hears the doorbell over the volume of the workout video she was doing in their den. She grabs her towel to pat her face, and drapes it around her neck. She picks up a bottle of water beaded up with condensation and takes a swig as she walks to the front door. She looks through the peephole and is taken aback by who she sees standing on the other side of the door.

She tears the front door open and stares in disbelief through the locked screen door. E-Tone locks eyes and admires his wife's beauty. There she stood, all 5'7" 165 lbs. of her. Standing there staring him in the face with her firm voluptuous breast in a black sports bra and with matching skin tight workout shorts hugging her round ass and wide hips. Her caramel brown skin was glistening with sweat. Her long brown hair pulled back in a ponytail. Her hazel eyes began to tear up as absolute joy consumed her. She unawaringly unlocks the screen door and falls into her soul mate's arms.

"Oh my God! I've missed you so much Eric! Please don't ever leave me again! I love you, I love you, I love you!" she says repeatedly while hugging and kissing her freshly returned husband.

"Sammy Pooh, I love you too baby! Daddy's home to stay Pooh! I ain't *goin* nowhere baby girl!" he replies as he carries her over the threshold of the doorway locking the door behind him.

He carries her directly to their bedroom upstairs, their lips and mouths exploring each other as if searching for lost treasure the whole way. He places her down on the edge of the bed.

"Baby let me take a shower first! I'm all sweaty!" says a semi reluctant Samantha.

"Don't worry *bout* no sweat, Sammy Pooh! I want to taste every flavor you have to offer me baby!" he says in a sensual tone, while he undresses his woman starting with her shoes and socks.

She stands up from her position on the bed and raises her arms. He removes the black sports bra exposing her large bronze breasts with erect nipples standing at attention, for him. He kisses and licks each nipple, starting with the left and then the right, gently cupping and massaging them in an alternating rhythm. While still sucking his wife's love globes, E-Tone removes her workout shorts and thong in a single motion. Samantha lifts her feet, one after the other, to step out of them. Completely naked, she sits down on the edge of the bed and unfastens his belt. E-Tone removes his Polo and t-shirt as she unbuttons his pants. He steps on the heels of his shoes and removes them without the help of his hands as she pulls his boxers down to his feet. He stands in front of his wife, totally nude, for the first time in months. She tenderly touches the scars on his stomach from the gunshot wound and surgery.

He comforts her by saying, "the doctors said they couldn't understand how I made it, but I wouldn't let myself die! All I kept thinking about was you and Junior and I couldn't give up! I love y'all too much to leave y'all here without me."

"Eric, I don't know how I would have maintained my sanity if you had died. Please don't put us through that again baby. I couldn't take it, my heart couldn't take it!" Samantha says before she engulfed his rock hard manhood.

He moans from the warmth and wetness of her throat. He cups the back of her head, grabbing her ponytail at the base, where the scrunchy held her long brown hair, and guides her as she takes all 10 inches of his love muscle in and out of her mouth. She scoots back on the bed with his extraordinary extremity still in her mouth and he follows her lead as she lays back. He repositions himself into the 69 position. The sweet musty smell mixed with the sultriness radiating from her slit of seduction, teased his sensations. He craved her taste like a bee craves honey. He licked slowly and teasingly at first causing her throat muscles to constrict around his penis. He continues to kiss and lick her inner thighs, pussy lips, and finally settling on her clit.

Orally pleasuring his woman with tongue techniques of a trained porn star, until a waterfall of cum flowed from her. Her body tremored and trembled as she came from his skillful display. Thinking of pleasing her, he held back his own eruption and repositioned them once again. He laid her on her left side, lifting her left leg, allowing him full access to entry. She tooted her ass in his direction to happily receive all of him, as he plunged into her.

"Ahhhhhh, I missed you daddy! I missed this dick! Fuck this pussy daddy! Mmmmmm, hit my spot daddy! Oh, right there! Get this pussy!" Samantha's vocal tirade was XXX worthy to say the least.

E-Tone dug in and out of his wife aggressively and ferociously, just like she loves to get fucked, until the tingling sensation of eruption overcame him and he exploded inside of her. He let out a low moan of pleasure indicating to his wife that the baby-making juices were escaping him. She quickly pushes him off her to suck the remaining fluids from his bell-head. Sucking and slurping dramatically to the point that "Lil Kim" would most likely blush. They continued to reconnect physically and emotionally throughout that afternoon, evening, and night, to the point of fatigue and exhaustion. They lay still in each other's arms as the sun rose.

Chapter 15

"From my estimation, it would be hard to make anything stick on the brother, especially since he was already incarcerated for close to a year when this part of the investigation ensued", says the senior DEA Agent, Pasoda.

"That's true, but we think that the younger brother only took over the organization when the older one got himself locked up!" Agent Millhouse retorts.

"Well, the burden of proof would be on us to validate that! And for that we need witnesses, which we don't have! I say we stick to nailing the players that are already on our radar. And if we get lucky and they wanna talk, then we go from there", explains Agent Pasoda as he looks at the pyramid of photos on their make-shift leader board.

"Just think, if Cardona hadn't been peddling pistols on the side, Homeland Security wouldn't have had this greedy son-of-a-bitch on their watch list to even notice that he was moving that much coke on the East coast! Talk about your lucky breaks! Now we have our eyes on the "Intrepido Guerrero" Cartel and three of their major outlet organizations. All because of one loose cannon. And to top it all off, he was willing to cooperate to avoid life in prison!" Agent Millhouse matter-of-factly states to his partner.

"Yeah, they don't make criminals like they used to! There's no honor amongst thieves anymore! There's absolutely no loyalty anymore! It's every criminal for himself. Once they get caught up and you throw some "football numbers" their way, 99% of them talk!" Pasoda vocalizes.

"Okay, so we're going to do a simultaneous three state bust? asked agent Millhouse.

"Well I guess that's why I'm the senior agent, besides the 20 years I got on you! Let me walk you through this. We bust Alverez once the semi-trucks leave California. We'll have men in place following the semis to their respective destinations. One in Texas, where we bust Santiago and his men, but the Ohio guy, Lewis, has a more complex set-up. He's got four hubs – three in the Ohio tri-state area and this new venture we're gonna spoil in Atlanta, "explains Agent Pasoda. Then he continues, "Once each truck arrives, we move on the players in that city, not allowing them to time to tip off the others. Is that plain enough for *yam*?" Agent Pasoda says with sarcasm to his younger, less experienced partner.

"Yeah, I got it loud and clear sir!" Agent Millhouse says in a smart-alek tone as he salutes.

"Very funny, wise guy. Now let's get these search warrants in order!" commands Agent Pasoda.

Meanwhile......

"How's the kid doing out there?" Vontez asked his business partners, Benard and Louis, as he arrives to the Raven's Rookie mini-camp a bit late.

"The kid's doing his thang out there! Catching, running, blocking, and pass protecting... he's looking like a seasoned veteran," Louis exclaimed.

"Looks like last year's starter might have some serious competition on his hands!" Bernard adds.

"That's what's up, I'm glad to hear that! Did you guys tell him what I wanted to talk to him about, regarding his plans after football?" says Vontez to his partners.

"Sure did, and to my surprise the kid wants to get into politics. Local at first, then nationally," Bernard replies.

"Yeah, the kid's sharp, man. A Political Science major. He had a 3.75 GPA and his parents are extremely socially conscious, so he has a great perspective on what's happening in the world today!" Louis conveys.

"Great, well I'm gonna stick around for a minute, but me and the girls are looking at a spot-on Martin Luther King Blvd in an hour. Urban Styles Barber and Beauty would make a great addition to this city as a business! Let's meet at the Burkshire Steakhouse at 8:00pm, bring the kid so we can talk!" Vontez communicates.

"It's on!" Bernard proclaims.

"That's what's up homie. See you and them fine ass women of yours tonight", Louis retorts.

When Louis, Bernard, and Logan arrive at Burkshire Steakhouse, Vontez, Stephanie and Keisha were already seated sipping on margaritas. Vontez stands as he sees the men approaching the table. He greets his friends and Bernard says "Logan, this is our associate, the one we told you about, Mr. Lewis".

"It's a pleasure to meet you Mr. Lewis", Logan says as he extends his hand to Vontez.

"Call me Tez young fella" Vontez replies as he returns the handshake.

Vontez then introduces Stephanie and Keisha as his ladies and Logan is taken aback. He looks in the direction of Louis and Bernard as if to gain confirmation, and in return they give him a 'don't even ask' look. The men all say 'hi' to the two beautiful women seated in front of them, before they take their respective seats.

After the first round of drinks and the appetizers were served, followed by meaningless small talk, Vontez brings up a serious topic.

"Logan, I know that your career is just getting started and for you, as a young man, it looks very, very promising! Here at MBK Sports Agency we are realists. The average NFL career is only 3 years and you must play five full seasons to be eligible for the NFL pension plan. And with the intensity of this violent sport, which we all love, everyone on that field is only one play away from a career ending injury. Here at MBK, we not only want you to be financially secure today, but with the right investments, we want to insure you are prepared for life after football. We live by our name 'My Brother's Keeper' and to that end, it is critical we do all we can for you from day one", Vontez shares with Logan.

"I'm happy to hear that sir!" Logan says with a smile.

"Call me Tez", reminds Vontez.

"Sorry Tez, as I was telling Benard and Louis, I was a political science major at Wake Forest. I have a real interest in the political arena", Logan informs him.

"Yes, so I've been told, that's great! Politics would be a great transition for you as an athlete. Kevin Johnson, Bill Bradly, Jesse Ventura, Reggie Williams and Steve Largent are all former athletes who made the transition to politics. Hell, even Charles Barkley considered it! The one thing those guys have in common are great public perceptions. No major drama or scandals young man. Hopefully you'll have a 15-year Hall of Fame career and you can make the same transition then, but until then you need to be visible in the community during the off-season. Maybe start a foundation to help disenfranchised inner-city youths", Vontez brainstorms on the fly.

"That sounds like a good idea; of course I'll run it by my parents first. But that sounds like a plan Tez!" Logan excitedly exclaims.

"There are many options available for you Logan, but I don't want you to lose focus on the primary goal at hand and that's making the team!" Vontez says, and the dinner party shares a laugh.

The women excuse themselves from the table to go to the ladies' room before the main course arrives. Logan takes the opportunity to ask Vontez a question that has been on his mind the entire evening.

"Excuse me Tez, I hope I'm not out of line by asking you this. Are you a pimp or something?"

The men all laugh and Vontez says, "That's a fair question Logan and I appreciate your candor and directness. No, I am not a pimp. I just happened to have stumbled across a living situation that suits me and the two women that I love. It's definitely a complex situation, but that's the simplified version of it. I'm not saying that our situation would work for everybody, but it certainly works for us," explains Vontez.

"I've been wanting to ask you that shit for years, but it's that simple, huh?" Louis says with skepticism.

"Damn Tez, you the truth! And the funny thing about it is that you don't flaunt it or come off as the least bit braggadocios about it. It's just you!" Bernard discerns.

"Well, I want to propose a toast....I know I just met you Tez, but I would like to make a toast to a man who got more game than Parker Brothers!" Logan says as he raises his glass.

"To Tez!" they all say in unison. That night they finished dinner, and all parties left satisfied with their relationships and mutual business agreements.

Chapter 16

It had been over a week since the joint closed casket memorial service for Sapphire and Jerome. Candy and Snake hadn't had a peaceful night's sleep in nearly a month. At first it was the worry and anxiety of their disappearance, and since the discovery of their bloated and decomposed corpses, their vivid imaginations were filled with violent and gruesome scenarios of their demise. Snake's guilt and new found morality was eating at him about the grisly murders of his cousin and his pregnant wife. One of the detectives on the case went to high school with Jerome and was extremely empathetic of the family's obvious grief and concerns.

Jerome's phone records were a closed part of the investigation and had led the detectives to a dead end, because the last phone number was to a burner phone with no name attached. After some coaxing, Snake was able to convince the detective that he might recognize the phone number if he were to see it. He did a helluva acting job persuading the detective that he didn't, when in actuality he knew whose number it belonged to once he viewed the phone log.

Snake kept the alarming but vital information to himself until he could confirm his own suspicions. His main focus now was to keep his family's mental and emotional state together. Candy was in shambles emotionally. The loss of her best friend whom she loved like a sister and her unborn baby was devastating to her soul. What was even more disturbing to here was the fact that even though they had changed and given their lives to Christ, Sapphire was still unable to escape the wretched hand of karma. Candy knew that when they were out hustlin and robbing niggas, what could be expected. She knew that at any given time, shit could get deep and pop off in a split second. But she just couldn't fathom something this diabolically disastrous happening once they had made their spiritual transformation. As Snake and Candy sat in the privacy of their home, she pours her heart out to him.

"I can't believe that she's gone. How could they do them like that! They didn't deserve it. She didn't deserve it! And to kill an innocent baby who ain't' never had a chance to do anything wrong, they're monsters! I don't know what's real anymore".

For the first time in her life, she had finally found real love! For the first time in her life she was happy. A new husband. A new baby. A new life! And now they're gone.

"There're all gone! Why! Why! Why!" Candy cries out as she slumps into Snake's comforting embrace.

Snake tries to find soothing words to give his woman the consoling she needs, but words eluded him. All he can do is hold her and stroke her back, while she continued to cry uncontrollably.

Later that evening, after he had settled Candy down, Snake left the house to follow his hunch. All of Jerome's licks had made an effort to contact him via messages left at the Snake Pit, but one, Reese! Reese was a Westside nigga who went to Jr. High School with Jerome, before he moved to the Eastside with his father. When he moved from the Westside neighborhood, which was "Crip" territory to the "Blood" territory of the Eastside, he had to get in where he fit in. He rose through the ranks in the "Blood" gang, because he was fearless and he could fight.

Snake knew that Reese would cop three to five bricks a week from Jerome. He did not come to the memorial service, and he hadn't left a message or tried to contact Snake about buying any dope, since Rome went missing. And when Snake recognized his number, he instantly put two and two together. He rationalized that Rome must have shown this *muthafucka* way too much, and that ultimately led to his and Sapphire's untimely and unfortunate demise. Although Snake was a new born again Christian, he couldn't help but to feel that he had to avenge his cousin's death. Fuck the money! This was about paying a debt of Loyalty that money couldn't buy and Reese was going to have to pay the note, with his life!

Chapter 17

"Baby, dinner's ready!" Regina yells as she carries the meatloaf on a serving platter from the kitchen to the dining room table.

Verdale grabs the twins from their play pen in the living room and meets his wife with a healthy grin, as he sees the meal that she has prepared for their small family. Meatloaf smothered in brown mushroom gravy, homemade garlic-ranch mashed potatoes, green beans and Hawaiian sweet rolls. The visual display was as appetizing as the tantalizing aroma that exuded from the still steaming food. They sit at the same end of the larger-than-average dining room table, with the twins seated side-by-side in their highchairs at the head of the table, flanked by a parent on either side of them. The kids sloppily ate their food, creating individual messes on their highchair trays. The proud parents of the pair marveled at their growing bundles of joy.

Regina, smiling brightly, starts the dinner conversation by asking, "How do you like it babe? I tried a new gravy recipe I saw online."

"Umm Umm, you put *yo* foot in this Babycakes! But of course, you always do." Verdale replied.

"I'm glad you like it", Regina chimes in. I know how we usually eat a red sauce with the meatloaf; I thought it was time to try something different. Speaking of something different Dale, your mom called me today" Regina says, slyly transitioning the topic of conversation.

"Oh yeah! What was she yapping' about babe?" He replies while taking another spoonful of the flavorful mashed potatoes, into his mouth.

"Dale she's worried about you. She told me about another one of those dreams she's had. She sounded pretty upset about it", she informs her husband.

"What else did she say?" he ponders aloud.

"She was basically telling me that she didn't want to alarm you or me, for that matter, but her uneasiness was growing and she wanted you to take her seriously. And I'm inclined to do just that, since I've heard the stories of your father and Tez. I don't want you to be next, Dale!" Regina explains to her husband.

"Gina, don't worry, babe. Everything's gonna be..." before he could finish his sentence, the doorbell rings, followed by a series of knocks.

"Were you expecting someone?" Regina asked.

"Nah, I ain't expecting nobody and don't nobody just pop over, I don't play that shit!" Verdale says while getting up from the table to answer the door.

Looking through the peephole first, his worst fears are realized. He opens the door to face Federal agents standing in front of him, brandishing a warrant for his arrest.

"Verdale Lewis we have a warrant for your arrest", the arresting agent stated before he started to read him his Miranda rights.

Regina peers around the corner just in time to see her husband being handcuffed.

"What's going on? Where are you taking my husband?" she cries out!

"Babe, call my lawyer!" Verdale manages to say before he is whisked off.

Reality set in as Regina closes the front door and enters the foyer of her home, feeling shaken and confused. The reality that her husband's loyalty to his brother had caught up to him. The reality that his mother's bad dreams had become their horrible reality. The reality that she didn't know how long it would be before she would see her husband without a prison uniform on. The reality that she was left alone to raise her twin toddlers.

The coordinated effort of the Federal Agents had simultaneously shut down pat of a cartel and had put a serious dent in the drug game nationwide. Major players, such as Fernando "Flash" Alverez, Juan Santiago, Verdale Lewis and several other men under their command were all under the watchful custody of the federal authorities. Who would stand firm? Who would choose their personal freedom and selfish interests over the "unspoken rules of the game?" The rule that plainly stated that you keep your mouth shut and let the police do their own dirty work!

Chapter 18

Snake ironically prayed for forgiveness for his transgressions before he committed his act of vengeance. Torn between what he knew was right and what he felt in his heart, he had made his decision. He made the decision to risk everything he had fought, lied and cheated to maintain, to bring the murderer of his cousin to swift street justice. He hadn't shaved or had a haircut since he'd made the connection between Reese and his cousin's death. He was a man on a mission, to say the least. Whether he was getting into character or trying to channel his "inner gangsta", Snake's appearance was a far cry from the "pretty boy" image he lauded. Hearing the nightly cries of his fiancé didn't help his feelings of anger and rage either. If anything, they added fuel to the fire of retribution that burned inside him.

With calm and patience, Snake watched Reese from a distance, seeing how he operated on a daily basis. He was enthused to know that Reese moved solo and was also a creature of habit. Tuesday, July 14th was the date Snake had planned to have marked on Reese's tombstone as the date of his death. He watched as he went to the local BW3's, for the Tuesday night wing special as he customarily did. Snake watched outside in a slider he had purchased especially for this mission. Once Reese got into his Ford 150, Snake knew that he would stop by the Marathon gas station and mini-mart for a gas fill-up and some cigarillos, before finally making his way home. He quickly drove to Reese's street, parked at the end and walked to the side of his modest house.

With a black backpack on his back and a chrome plated pistol in hand, Snake had to admit that this cat was low-key. If he hadn't known firsthand what he was copping, he would have never guessed that this *muthafucka* was buying bricks. He never brought women or licks back to his home, always taking care of business away from where he laid his head. He wasn't flashy or drove expensive cars or wore gaudy jewelry. He was definitely under the radar.

Snake continued to wait patiently, but he didn't have to wait long before Reese pulled up. He got out of his truck and before he could reach the front door, Snake crept up on the porch right behind him, with the pistol pointed to his back.

"Don't make a sound or it will be the last sound you make *muthafucka*!" he snarled, then commanded him to open the door.

"Please don't kill me! Man, take what you want! I got $2,500.00 on me man. It's yours, that's all I got!" Reese begged.

"Shut the fuck up nigga!" Snake yells and shoots him the back of the leg.

The muffled sound from the 9mm with the silencer was even more drowned out by the screams of pain from Reese as he fell to the floor.

"Put your hands behind *yo* back nigga!" Snake yelled.

Reese did as he was told and Snake took some rope from the backpack and tied his hands behind him.

"Get up on your feet *muthafucka!*" he orders Reese, who limps and hobbles to finally stand.

Snake directs him to the basement door and pushes the wounded man with his hands tied behind his back, down the stairs. The padded, carpeted steps provide a bit of cushion to help break his fall, and he remains conscious. Snake scurries down the stairs after him. He grabs Reese up and directs him to sit in a wooden chair that was in his sight. Still woozy from the fall, Reese finally looks up to see Snake's face.

"Snake, man what the fuck? I ain't have *nothin* to do with what happen to Rome! Man, I swear to God!" he pleads.

"See, how the fuck you know why I'm here!" Snake says loudly as he continues to secure him with rope to the chair.

Snake smacks him on the side of his face with the gun, causing blood to spurt from the gash left behind.

"I'm gonna ask you two questions and If I get the right answers nigga, I might let yo punk ass live! Why you kill my people and where's my dope *muthafucka!*" Snake growls through gritted teeth.

"Snake, it wasn't me!" implores Reese. "Wrong answer *muthafucka!*"

And Snake shoots him in the other leg. Snake puts a gag in his mouth and goes in the backpack to pull out a small battery powered rotary saw.

"Now, this is how this shit's gonna go nigga! I already know that you was the last *muthafucka* to talk to my people. It's been weeks and you ain't tried to buy shit from me or even inquire about shit! So, I know you had something to do with it! I'ma start cutting off toes until you tell me what I wanna hear!" Snake shouts like a man possessed.

He fires up the rotary saw and pulls off Reese's right shoe and sock. He slices off the big toe and Reese lets out a blood curdling squeal. "You ready now, *muthafucka*?!" Snake yells with fire in his eyes.

Reese shakes his head yes, and Snake loosens the gag that was tightly tied around his mouth and head.

"Snake you crazy man! You done cut off my toe!" cries Reese.

Snake hastily puts the gag back in his mouth. "*Muthafucka* I thought you had something important to say! Snake angrily spews, and starts the saw back up.

He proceeds to cut off the other four toes on that foot in one swipe.

"You got something you wanna say now nigga?" He solicits a response from a now cowering Reese, who shakes his head up and down signaling yes.

Snake again pulls the gag out of his mouth and slides it down his chin.

"I wasn't planning on killing 'em man, I swear!" Reese pleads.

"What the fuck happened? And where is my shit!" yells Snake.

"Look man, I was gonna buy my regular when he pulls out a big ass bag full of bricks! I ain't never seen that much dope in my life! The greed got the best of me cause when he was counting the money, I pulled out my burner! I was just gonna rob 'em and get out of town, but he went for my gun. I didn't know his girl was home, but I guess she must've heard us tussling and came in the room. She hopped on my back and was scratching at my face while me and him was still fightin' for control of the gun. Man, before I knew it, the gun went off and Rome was hit in the stomach. I threw her off my back and smacked her with the pistol. I didn't realize that Rome was still conscious, but he came charging at me so I shot 'em again. I couldn't leave her alive man, she would've ratted me out! So, I ransacked the house looking for the money. I knew he had to have some paper in there, with all those bricks he had", boldly says Reese.

"Dumb ass nigga! That was my shit!" Snake roars and smacks him across the head with the butt of the gun. "Why you move their bodies? Tell me that!" Snake demands.

"I figured I could get rid of the bodies and get rid of any evidence against me. I know she had my DNA under her fingernails. I panicked!" exclaims Reese.

"Where is my shit at nigga?" yells Snake.

"If I tell you, then you gonna kill me! I ain't stupid!" bellows Reese.

"There's a 50 – 50 shot I will, but if you don't, there's a 100% chance you gone die! Nice and slow!" Snake says diabolically.

After torturing Reese for over an hour, cutting off his left foot one toe at a time, he finally breaks, directing Snake to the floor safe by the furnace, where he finds 27 bricks still wrapped up, and $600,000. Snake removes the contents and dumps them in a trash bag.

"Snake, I know you gone kill me! Please just make it quick!" Reese begs, as he had come to terms with death.

"Fair enough!" Snake answers him and presses the 9mm to the side of his head and squeezes the trigger, putting Reese out of his misery and ending the night of terror.

Chapter 19

Mama V was sad yet relieved that her son was locked up in a Federal Penitentiary. Rationalizing that at least he was in a safe place. And if he had to be locked up, a Federal institution was better than a state run facility any day of the week. Her nightmares had stopped as abruptly as the Federal agents had knocked at her son's door. Although they were still early on in the court proceedings, everyone throughout the various organizations had remained firm, including Fernando Alverez's and Juan Santiago's men. What seemed like an air-tight case at first glance was purely circumstantial and based on the sole cooperation and testimony of their star witness, Rodolfo Cardona. No one else was willing to rat out the heads of their organizations, no matter how much time they were threatened with.

The workers who were directly involved, via being caught red-handed unloading the product, were mostly ill-legal immigrants who barely spoke English, a commonality that each organization had. It was an unspoken rule and key factor in keeping their business inconspicuous. How could the men tell information that they didn't understand? As far as the men who supervised the laborers and who received the shipments, they were facing stiffer penalties, mainly because the Feds were trying to put added pressure on them to talk. But, their lawyers were very well compensated to represent them, and their families were safe. Once Fernando figured out who the snitch was, he got word via his lawyer to his uncle, to have him silenced for good. Fortunately for him, he never purchased any firearms from Cardona or he would've been up shit creek without a paddle.

Worst case scenario, the men were looking at up to 10 years a piece for conspiracy charges. With good behavior and programs that would be more like 7.5 years, which was a lot better than the life sentences they were looking at if Cardona made it to the witness stand. Luckily Verdale had the gift of foresight, putting his rental properties and janitorial businesses in his wife's name, just in case of a situation such as this.

Regina's worst fears had been realized. What she always feared, since Verdale had taken over for his brother, had come to fruition. Once Mama V had voiced her concern about her dreams to Regina, anxiety and worry had overwhelmed her. Now that Verdale was going to physically be away from his family for an extended period of time, she wished she had someone to lean on, much like Stephanie and Kiesha had when Vontez was away. Being a single parent was something that she had never pictured for herself, but she had every intention of remaining loving and loyal to her husband.

Vontez was also upset about his brother's unfortunate circumstance, as well as Tae and Lil Dee's confinement due to their involvement. He knew what this gangsta life had to offer, but he never wanted these end results for the ones he cared about. Knowing that his brother was solid financially, he got power of attorney over Tae and Dee's assets, to ensure that they would be financially secure upon their release. Their devotion and allegiance to him had far exceeded a mere business relationship, they were his extended family and he would treat them as such.

E-Tone had gotten in contact with Vontez, letting him know that he was sorry for not completing his assigned task. Vontez let him know that it was all good and that he was sorry for the loss of J.J. The two men brought each other up to speed about where they were at in their lives, both expressing their appreciation for the other for years of a great mutually beneficial relationship. E-Tone expressed his concern for Verdale and his legal troubles and extended his hand and services to help in any way. Vontez respectfully declined, but asked was there anything that E-Tone needed. E-Tone let him know that because of him, he was in a comfortable position to survive and provide for his family.

Since their initial meeting, Logan Williams had taken Vontez's advice and had started a Foundation based in the Baltimore, Maryland area. The Logan's League Foundation was an organization that targeted inner-city youth with a focus on education. They provided back to school supplies and after school tutoring programs. They also implemented a before school breakfast program, as well as provided a hot meal to the students who attended their after school tutoring program. They realized that it was very hard for impoverished children to learn when they were hungry or worried about where they might get their next meal. Logan, who had dreams and aspirations to become a political candidate, was well on his way to making an impact both on and off the field.

Chapter 20

Cindy Sinclair stood in the doorway admiring her daughter Candy as the makeup artist and hair stylist doted over her, putting the finishing touches on the stunning bride to be. Tears welled up in her eyes as she thought back to the many years she spent in the streets as a dope-fiend and prostitute, missing out on valuable time in the life of her beautiful daughter. Tears of regret, because she wasn't there to help guide and nurture her; But also tears of joy because she was happy and proud that her daughter had somehow managed to find love and happiness despite her parental shortcomings.

Candy stood up from the styling chair located in the dressing room of the wedding banquet center, where her and Snake's wedding and reception was about to be held.

"How do I look, Ma?" she asked while till looking in the full-length mirror.

"You look beautiful! Simply beautiful baby! I wish your grandmother was here to see you, but I know she's looking down from heaven, smiling from ear to ear." She replies while dabbing her eyes with a tissue.

"I wish my girl Sapphire was here, but I know she looking down from heaven too, holding her baby, smiling and happy for me. I'm so happy that she got saved, before...well, you know," she says while getting misty eyed. Her mother walks over to comfort her.

"Come on now baby don't cry. You gonna mess up that pretty make-up Candy. God got a plan for all of us and don't worry yourself trying to figure it out. Just be happy and enjoy this day that God got planned for you! You hear me!?" Cindy says with motherly affection and love.

"Yes ma'am. Mama I'm so happy that you're here to share this day with me!" Candy says as she hugs her mama tightly.

"Baby I wouldn't have missed this for the world," says Cindy while returning the embrace.

Her bridesmaids, Precious, Fawn, Monique, Joyce and Juanita enter the room through an adjoining door attached to their shared dressing room. The women share hugs and compliments with one another with them all fawning over how gorgeous Candy looked in her wedding dress, before the wedding coordinator told everyone to take their places outside the ballroom entrance. Candy waited in the dressing room for her cue, so she wouldn't run into Snake before the ceremony began. That would be bad luck and they had experienced enough bad luck along their journey to happiness; there was no need to chance anymore.

Tiny, Chubbs, Virgil, Larry and Calvin were the groomsmen who walked the ladies down the aisle, followed by a handsome and dapper Snake, who was dressed in an all-white Marc Jacobs custom tuxedo with matching white loafers.

After everyone had walked down the aisle, including the flower girl and ring bearer, the wedding coordinator knocked on Candy's dressing room door. Cindy and Candy emerged arm in arm. Cindy was honored that her only daughter had asked her to give her away. They stood at the entrance, as John Legend's "All of me" started to play they proceeded to walk slowly down the aisle, admiring the beautiful decorations and the many people in attendance. Snake stood poised yet nervous, as Candy and her mother walked toward him.

"Who gives this woman to this man?" asked Rev. Jackson.

"I do" says Cindy. Snake then hugs and kisses his future mother-in-law.

He takes Candy's hand and they both turn to face the minister. Rev. Jackson conducts a traditional wedding ceremony until they get to the wedding vows, where both Candy and Snake have prepared their own.

Candy states in a loud, clear voice, "Pernell Andre' Collins, you've shown me what true unconditional love is, and in addition to that love, your supportive and nurturing nature has made me fall in love with you, time and time again. You are the man of my dreams, as well as my reality and I feel so fortunate, honored and blessed to be able to spend the rest of my life with you. Today, I vow to you that I will always be the woman that you love and respect. To treat you with love, honor and loyalty. And to always represent you with the utmost dignity, until death do we part!" Tears slowly run down her face as she finishes.

"Candy Lanae Sinclair, ever since our first date, I have known that you were the woman that I had been searching for. I'm so amazingly happy that God saw fit to bring you in my life. At times, I feel undeserving of your love, but I know that God doesn't make mistakes and that's why I vow to you on this day, Saturday August 29, 2015 to always love, honor, respect, and protect you until my very last breath. To always show you the compassion and understanding you deserve. To support and encourage your dreams and to always remain loyal to you, until death do us part," Snake says with total humility and compassion.

By this time most of the ladies and a few men had tears rolling down their faces from the heartfelt words of the two.

Rev. Jackson steps forward and says, "the rings please." After the rings were exchanged and a prayer offered, he continues by saying, "I now pronounce you man and wife. You may kiss your bride!"

The family and friends in attendance erupt in applause. The Reverend continues after the couple kiss, "ladies and gentlemen it is my esteemed honor to introduce to you for the very first time, Mr. and Mrs. Pernell Andre' Collins!" and the rapturous applause continues as the couple walks down the aisle toward the ballroom's front entrance.   Once outside the ballroom the couple pauses for a moment to take it all in.

"You look sexy as hell Mrs. Collins." Snake seductively states to his brand-new wife.

"You don't look so bad yourself, Mr. Collins!" she coyly replies.

The wedding coordinator comes to the hallway to direct the couple to re-enter the ballroom and take their seats at the table that has replaced the wedding gazebo on the center stage. Snake had spared no expense for the wedding with T-bone steaks, Lobster Tails and Roasted Garlic Chicken being the three main course options.   The wedding cake was a five-tier red velvet master-piece, created by the "Cake Boss".   And to top it off, Snake had hired DJ Kid Capri to set the party mood for the evening.

During the portion of the reception when the best man and maid-of-honor were to make their toasts and speeches, a slideshow honoring Jerome and Sapphire graced the big screen in the ballroom.   Tears flowed throughout the ballroom as images of their passionate love affair were displayed. After the screen faded to black, Snake stood up and raised his glass to propose a toast.

"To Jerome and Sapphire! May they rest in Peace!" and echoes of, "to Jerome and Sapphire" cascaded throughout the ballroom.

Candy and Snake walked to the dance floor as DJ Kid Capri announced the first dance. Frankie Beverly and Maze's "We Are One" began to play over the sound system. They held each other closely, swaying rhythmically to the smooth groove as the onlookers marveled at the handsome couple. The day went completely as planned without a hitch. From the first dance, to the cutting of the cake, a bombarded gift table, to the soul train line that included everyone, young and old.

The happy couple said their goodbyes to everyone. Friends and family gathered at the entrance tossing uncooked rice, as they exited the banquet center to enter the awaiting stretched limo. As the limousine pulled off onto the main road that led to the expressway on their way to the airport for the honeymoon, Snake leaned over and kissed his glowing bride.

"Candy-cane I love you so much and I'm ready to give up this street life, so we can live happily ever after. Baby, I'm tired of having to look over my shoulder!" Snake sincerely says to his newly wedded wife.

"You don't know how happy you've made me! Pernell Andre' Collins. I love you with all my heart and will until the day I die!" she replies, and they kiss with the passion of a couple in love.

The car stops on the side of the road. The limo driver hits the power sliding glass divider while they were still engrossed in their tongue wrestling match.

"Ahh, don't y'all make a fine couple!"

The couple is startled by the sound of a familiar voice. They turn to see E-Tone with a 40-caliber handgun pointed at them. They both freeze in a calm terror, as they realize that the chickens had come home to roost. He shoots Snake in the forehead killing him instantly and Candy screams in horror as blood and brain matter splatter all over her.

E-Tone diabolically states, "It's not gonna be that easy for you Ms. Candy. I'm gonna have fun with yo ass!"

Then he hits the button closing the tinted divider window. She struggles to open the doors but then realizes the child locks are activated. She tries to kick the windows out, but grows exhausted because they are bullet proof. She loses all hope of escape. Her betrayal and disloyalty had finally caught up with her, she realizes. She looks at her husband's dead body slumped next to her and comes to the realization that this too would be her fate. Candy smiles a twisted smile of relief and bows her head to pray, understanding that the only loyalty that mattered now was her loyalty to her Lord and Savior.

The End

PSST..........

Turn the page for a sneak peak of Vontez's book:

"The Life and Times of Vontez"

The Introduction

"I now pronounce you Man and Wife! You may now kiss your bride", said Pastor Mike as Saprina and I look into each other's eyes.

The happiest day of my born-again life didn't come by mistake, but by Gods design! At age 43 and entering into my second and final marriage, I've experienced some love, pain, joy, and heartache. But all that I've been through, good, bad, and indifferent has molded me into the God-fearing, responsible family man that I am today. Coupled with a deep appreciation for the simple things in life, such as being able to come home from a hard days' work to prepare dinner with my woman for my 11-year old step-daughter, and our 1-year old son, to be able to sit in the living room and eat that same meal, while sitting beside my loyal Queen, and watch the reality shows that flood our airwaves. Yeah, it sounds so trivial, simple, or downright boring, but that's me now. A far cry from the man I once was.......someone who just wants to blend in with the crowd, so different from my younger counterpart, who was quite the contrary......but sooner or later we all have to grow up!

"Barbara, where are you going", Grandma Daisy yelled.

"Down the street with Bobbie Mama", said a 14-year old Barbara who was already looking like a woman 4 years her senior.

"Make sure your rump is in this house by the time the street lights come one", Grandma Daisy said in a stern voice.

"Yes ma'am", Barbara said as she closed the front door making sure she shut the screen door behind her.

Now growing up in the 60's and early 70's, Barbara was a typical teenager always trying to keep up with the latest trends, dances and slang, but being brought up in a semi-strict Christian household (her father being an old school Southern Baptist preacher) she learned a dual existence. She acted one way around her parents and took on another persona around her friends.

"Where your sister Roy?" Barbara politely asked.

"She in *da* house", said a cat-eyed 16 year old Roy, who was already making a name for himself as a heart and law breaker.

"Where that dog at Roy? You know I'm scared of dogs", Barbara whined.

"Girl quit being so scary, he in the back tied up. And you ain't scared of no dogs *messin* with that nigga Pee-Wee", he snickered. "That's why you *fillin* out like *dat!*"

Barbara blushed *cause* she, like so many of Bobbie's friends, also had a secret crush on him.

"Whatever!" Barbara said as she made her way up the stairs to the front door, instinctively switching her newly found weapon from side to side, and Roy, being a 16 year old bundle of hormones, enjoyed every minute of it.

In his best *"Mack Daddy"* impression, Roy smoothly blurted out, "I see you *draggin* a lil *sumthin* in that wagon girl!"

Barbara giggled thinking to herself that every young dude she knew wanted to be a pimp. Bobbie, hearing the front door open, peeked from the kitchen to see who it was.

"Hey girl", she said with a smile beaming from her face, happy to see her bestie. "You hungry?" Bobbie asked as the smell of fried bologna filled the house.

"Hell yea", Barbara said, already reaching for the white bread and mayo sitting on the table.

Now Barbara and Bobbie shared the same first name, but Bobbie loved her nick name. They looked like salt and pepper shakers standing next to one another. Barbara, being the color of hot chocolate, getting her complexion from the Alabama bred Southern preacher, and Bobbie, being a high yellow-reddish tint, shared by both her mother and father. And on top of that, their personalities complemented one another; Bobbie being the shit talker, a trait Barbara admired after always having to be the tame quite church girl. But, Barbara being a natural fighter, being the baby of five other girl siblings in the house, always had her shit talking girlfriend's back, being that she was often biting off more than she could chew. Yeah, Barbara and Bobbie were two peas in a pod back then!

120

"What you *wanna* do today?" Barbara asked taking a bite of the fried swine sandwich.

"Girl, you know, talk shit, swallow spit and don't give these niggas a lil bit!" Bobbie said as the girls shared a laugh.

"Girl, you and *yo* brother been watching too many pimp movies!" Barbara said as she snickered.

"You see, all they *wants* is the "*honey*", and all I *wants* is the money", Bobbie said in her best Pretty Tony voice. Their giggles continued and they finished their food.

"I need to take a shower", Bobbie stated. "I smell like I work at a diner or something. Girl, give me like fifteen minutes".

"It's cool", said Barbara. "I'll watch T.V."

After gathering up her toiletries and hygiene products, Bobbie goes in the bathroom to shower up while Barbara sits in the living room to watch "*Soul Train*", the *hippest trip* on Television. Roy comes into the house to see a ripe Barbara trying to get the steps down to the latest dance, *"the hustle"*.

"I see you lil mama", Roy says upon entering the house *wit* his dog on a leash, a brindle boxer, his dog of choice.

Barbara stiffens with fear at the sight of the canine.

"Boy, hold that dog. Roy, I ain't *playin*! Barbara says sternly, but not too loud as to upset the tail *waggin* beast.

"I got him. Damn, you scared *fo'real* ain't *cha*?" Roy asks.

"Hell yeah. I don't like *'em* one bit"! Barbara quickly replied.

"Well, I'll take him back out back if I can get a kiss", Roy said playingly.

"Stop *playin'* Roy", Barbara said with a fearful look in her eye.

Roy took two steps closer.

"Stop *playin'* Roy, please!" begged Barbara.

"Huh, what's that? I can't hear you", Roy said taking advantage of the curvaceous teen's phobia while inching closer.

"ok, ok", pleaded Barbara.

Roy, seeing the look of terror in the young girl's eyes, mixed with a hint of a young girl's crush, he made a hasty retreat outside to tie up the mut. Upon his return, Barbara's look of relief that the must was no longer present was clearly apparent, and Roy grabbed her by the hand and led her upstairs.

"Just one kiss Roy", Barbara said, her voice still cracking from the moments prior.

Well one kiss lead to two, three, and four, and when Barbara wanted to stop, Roy's threats of getting the dog on her kept Barbara frozen in fear. Rigid and uncontesting, Barbara laid there, a victim of rape by her best friend's brother whom she once *crushed on*, but with each hump of his 5'7" slim frame, a hate formed instantly; One that would spill over into the seed, which he was planting in the fertile 14 year old ground of Barbara's womb. That seed of fear, hate, and lust was me. Ronald; Named after the boyfriend whom she was involved with, Pee Wee. Thus, begins my life, not conceived out of love and affection, but out of pure unadulterated carnal desire.....and here begins the story of Ron C!